THE ISLAND RULES?

TIM DAVIS

PENNY CRESS

The Island Rules? / by Tim Davis

www.timdaviscreations.com

Summary: Creatures of the land and sea are set against each other in a plot to change the rules of the Island

ages 7-12

Star field obtained from: kjpargeter / Freepik

Orions Belt Constellation from GoodStock

Cover design by Tim Davis

Pennycress Publishing

Greenville, SC 29609

ISBN: 9780998943589

With gratitude to my friends at the
Highlights Foundation, offering
"intimate and inspiring workshops
for children's authors and illustrators."
I began writing this story under the
influence of their magic, and couldn't
stop until I'd finished.

Other books by Tim Davis

Mice of the Herring Bone

Mice of the Nine Lives

Mice of the Seven Seas

Mice of the Westing Wind (Book One)

Mice of the Westing Wind (Book Two)

Tales from Dust River Gulch

More Tales from Dust River Gulch

The Island Rule

Mort and the Sour Scheme

Mort Finds his Roots: Mushrooms in the Wild

Mort's Circle

Author's Note

Underground is a great place to hide things. Secrets held in ancient wonders buried in the deep challenge us to rethink some of our most basic ideas—perhaps even correct our errors.

In the dark, we can learn to see in new ways. So much information is gathered by sight, we often consider our vision the sense that's most reliable. But in *The Island Rules?* some creatures see what they want to see or miss something right in front of their eyes. Hidden objects in the cave drawings might give our heroes the clues they're looking for. But nature is also full of distracting patterns leading us to believe something that may not be as it seems.

In *The Island Rule,* action happened mostly in daylight. But this second story of the Island series spends more time underground. Try to imagine what might be hiding in those dark places you can't see.

Table of Contents

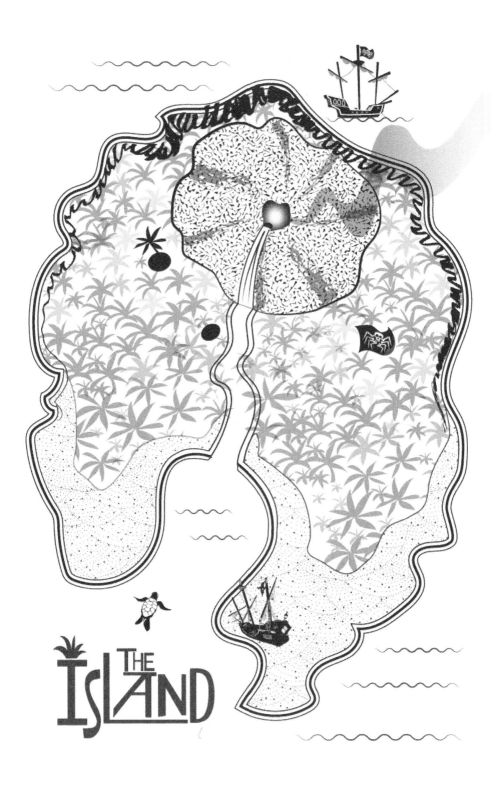

THE ISLAND

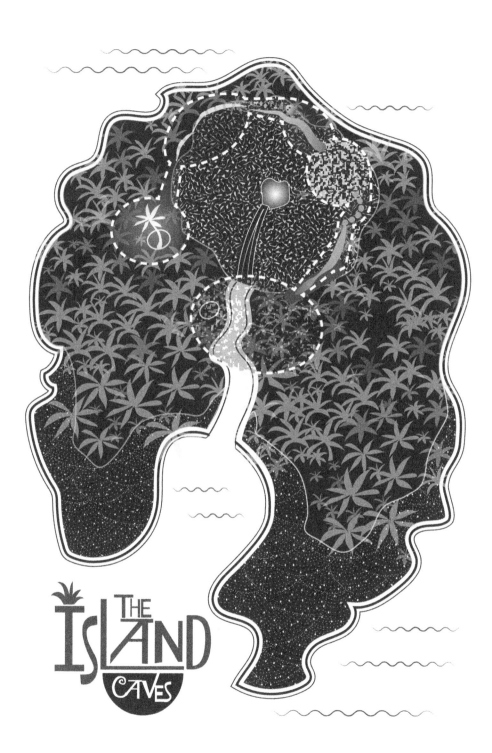

THE ISLAND CAVES

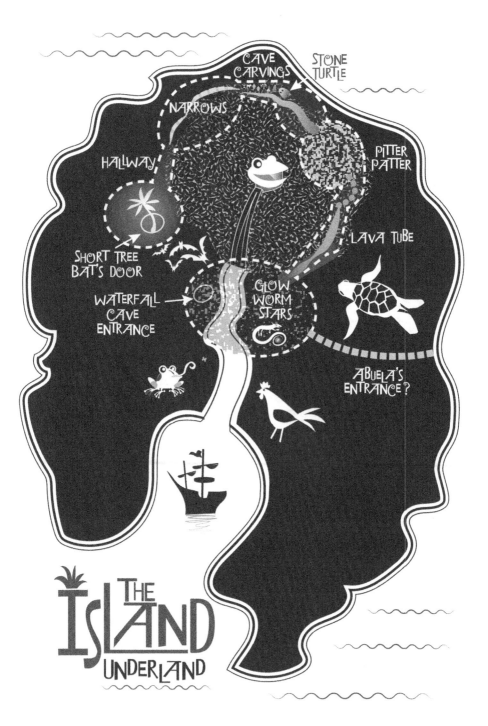

PROLOGUE

THE BELLY OF THE VOLCANO

It belched. Like a huge black snake slithering up from the depths and escaping into the sea. Molten rock bubbled up and over the volcano's mouth. Lava poured down its lips. It steamed, sizzled, and streamed down through the rain forest like a giant glowing blob, digesting the palm trees in flames along the banks of the stream toward the bay.

Boulders fell from the volcano's narrow upper face, crashing into the forest below. Would it explode? The island creatures fled to the beach and trembled in fright. Waiting . . . waiting. But the ground stopped shaking. Was it done? Was it over? The cloud above it was small, and swept away by the winds of the sea. So the island was not covered in hot ash. Apparently it was only a burp of fiery indigestion. The volcano had

1

slept so long—simmering with a lazy plume of haze for as long as the island creatures could remember. Now it had awakened.

Sunlight breaking through the haze, every eye stared intently at the peak of the great volcano. Every ear listened—hoping for silence—hoping the mountain would return to its slumber. Nothing could have prepared them for the sight that emerged through the still wrinkling heated air. A face! A face in the rock! All eyes searched the crowd of creatures huddled along the beach. All looked for one of their number. For that face.

"It's the gecko! It's Jajumbee!"

Chapter 1

The End of the Island?

In the purple light just before sunrise, Jajumbee the gecko and his plump friend Boofo the treefrog walked and hopped along the beach. The sand cooled their toes, and Boofo's belly. It was the only peace the gecko had enjoyed for hours. He was out of sorts, since everyone seemed to be whispering about his . . . and the volcano's . . . face.

A sand crab popped from his hole and sidestepped over to them. "How can this be?" asked Carlos, pointing back toward the mountain. "The volcano—it looks like you!"

The gecko closed his eyes and put his hand to his forehead. It stuck. He sighed, then released the suction at the tips of his fingers. "They see what they want to see," he answered, wiping the back of his hand over his eyes. "Patterns in nature. We see them all around us!" Jajumbee gestured out toward the waves of the sea. "Is that a turtle? Or just a wave? Anything can look like something else."

"I suppose," said the crab, "But other creatures— they think it's a sign—a sign from below."

"A sign?" exclaimed the gecko, one eyebrow raised. "Of what?"

Carlos shrugged his oversized front claws. "Who knows? Maybe the end of the Island as we know it." His eye stalks raised at the very thought of it.

"Island doom?" croaked Boofo. He was a frog of few words, and he wanted even those two back as soon as he had spoken them.

Jajumbee hung his head and sighed again.

"Sorry, Jajumbee."

"It's not your fault, Boofo." Jajumbee patted his friend's orange and black spotted shoulder. "Even my songs—no one sings them no more."

4

"Your songs," croaked the treefrog, "the best."

Carlos clicked along beside them. His eye stalks lowered, and he shielded his mouth so no one else could hear him. "They are afraid," he whispered.

The three sat in the sand watching a pink dawn paint the gentle waves lapping onto the beach. But the beach was now blackened by the cooled lava all along the banks of the stream.

A young sea turtle's head popped up from the water in front of them—bobbing gently in the bay. Then her shell emerged, looking like a stone crafted with painted tiles.

"Zani!" The sight of his sea friend seemed to give Jajumbee a glimmer of hope again.

"You see?" muttered Carlos. "It *was* a turtle."

Panzanilla—Zani for short—shook herself and crawled onto the sand.

The gecko was eager for her report. "The bay, how is it changed?"

"Changed?" Zani responded, "Yes, much changed! Part of the reef is covered over now, as smooth as black glass. Much easier to navigate."

Throwing his claws up, Carlos complained, "The reef was a shield against ships—like the wreck that covered my hole in the sand."

"The volcano just rolled out a welcome mat to the sea," Jajumbee said. "So the Island is now open for visitors."

Boofo's eyes widened at the thought of what that could mean, especially after all the trouble they'd had with that pirate ship, the one with the spider flag.

Carlos just grumbled and clicked his claws.

"I was a visitor too," Zani reminded her friends.

Sunrise looked like a fiery halo behind Zani's head. And just as quickly, a rooster crowed from the edge of the forest. He crowed again and again, seeming to love the sound of his own voice.

Carlos covered his ears and skittered back to his hole in the beach, tossing up sand as he dropped into it.

"Rosie's kid, always crowing." Zani narrowed her eyes and pulled a face toward her friends.

"Too much!" added Boofo.

Jajumbee sighed as Chanty, the young rooster, stole the peace of the moment again.

6

Zani moved to the place where Carlos had been. "The creatures are worried. The volcano's eruption set them on edge," she said.

"It's like they don't feel at home on the Island anymore," Jajumbee agreed. "And this is the only home they have ever known!"

"Island home," Boofo agreed.

"Maybe the Island has its own answers?" said Zani.

"Some way for everyone to better appreciate the very ground they stand on," added Jajumbee.

Zani continued, "In the caves . . . remember? The drawings we saw on the walls?"

Boofo nodded. "Island stories!"

"Yes," agreed Zani. "Our history."

"Where I dropped our torch and we were left in the dark," Jajumbee remembered, "I was so surprised to see. . . "

"You," croaked Boofo, "you and your stew."

Jajumbee was known for his Blessing stew, made from all good things that the Island gave. Even that was inscribed on the cave walls.

"Those drawings—are they more than ancient history? . . . Maybe they're a key to the future, too?" Zani wondered.

"We should go back to take another look," Jajumbee said. "Perhaps those drawings in the dark could enlighten creatures up here. Give us the answers we need."

"But," he continued, "what will everyone think if I go down into the caves—into the very heart of the volcano they say now looks like me?"

"Who knows?" Boofo shrugged. "But they leave you alone."

"Will you two go with me?" the gecko asked.

"Not my face," answered Boofo, looking toward the volcano. "Too dark. No mosquitoes. Not again."

"I understand, my friend." Jajumbee nodded. "Perhaps it's best you stay above. Something's brewing here on the surface, too—maybe even more dangerous than the volcano."

Boofo's eyes got bigger at the very thought of it. "More dangerous?"

"Yes. Mistrust and division are spreading."

Zani raised a flipper. "I'll go with you, Jajumbee."

8

"Thank you, my friend. The mountain may be calling me, but I'd rather not go alone."

Then Jajumbee remembered a song.

> *Pit, pit. Pit, pitter, patter.*
> *Go down, See what's the matter.*
> *Who knows? Follow the water.*
> *Could be, that's how we got here.*

> *Pit, pit. Pit, pitter, patter.*
> *Goes down, down goes the water.*
> *In caves, in lower places,*
> *Follow the path it traces.*

CHAPTER 2

BAT'S DOOR

The Island offered two entrances into the caves below—well, the creatures knew of two. One was known to the surface dwellers as the Short Tree. A great palm growing from the cave floor reached up into the light of the forest, offering a sort of ladder to come and go. Underneath, it was simply called the Bat's Door—for obvious reasons.

The other way to the caves was not named, but it was how Zani had entered them when she'd first arrived—flushed down into an underground pool in the midst of a storm. There she had met Solo, the blind salamander. He seemed to prefer the solace he found there, as well as the tasty glow worms that dropped from the ceiling.

The three friends looped around the common streamside paths to avoid as many creatures as they could along the way. No other crabs spotted them. A couple of sparkling hummingbirds flew down to take a look, but quickly darted away without a word.

"I hope they don't tell anybody they saw us out here," said Jajumbee.

"Few words," croaked Boofo, "like me."

"More trustworthy that way." Zani winked at Boofo, who blushed a brighter shade of orange.

Jajumbee agreed. "That's why we need you to stay above," the gecko assured the treefrog. "You've always been a faithful friend. We'll make an agreement with Emilio. If anything goes wrong up here—if you need to contact us—tell him. Send out a high-pitched croak. He'll find us and let us know."

"Big ears," smiled Boofo.

"And nobody flies better through dark places," added Jajumbee.

Meanwhile, Zani gathered berries as the group made their way through the underbrush of ferns and wildflowers. She folded the snacks into a large leaf and tucked them into a corner of her shell. A careful search finally yielded the perfect stick for a torch. Jajumbee

12

wrapped the end in dried leaves and slathered them in the thickest tree sap he could find. Boofo captured a few small items with timely flicks of his long, sticky tongue—even a crunchy-looking dragonfly!

"Good roasted!" he exclaimed.

Zani had her doubts, but Jajumbee accepted every gift gratefully, even some mushrooms dislodged by the treefrog's misses.

At last, in a small clearing—there it was! Wide palm leaves spread over a gaping hole in the ground.

"Short Tree!" exclaimed Boofo.

"Or Bat's Door," said Jajumbee, "it all depends on your point of view."

"And ours will soon be from below," added Zani.

The gecko faced his treefrog friend. "Boofo."

"Yes."

"Emilio might be sleeping, but can you give your highest-pitched croak—right down—down into the hole?"

Boofo cleared his throat—stretching it out like a bubble, then deflating it again, until he was ready. He closed his eyes and leaned just over the edge.

"Squeeeeee . . . ." his croak rose higher and higher in pitch until Zani and Jajumbee could hear it no more.

But Emilio did. Before long a large furry-faced gray bat flapped out the Bat's Door and presented himself to the three friends.

"You called for meee?" asked Emilio. "Why wake me up at such an hour?" His eyes squinted in the morning light.

Jajumbee announced, "So sorry, but thank you, my friend! We . . . the whole Island . . . may need your help . . ."

The bat's eyes opened all the way now. "Yes, I wondered when you'd come!"

He squeaked a bit from the Island's most famous song:

> *Bat in the cave and fish in the school,*
>
> *Nobody break-a thee Island Rule,*
>
> *First you must give, and then you can take,*
>
> *Nobody break-a thee Island Rule,*
>
> *Nobody break-a thee Island Rule!*

14

Then he added, "I'm ready to geeve what I can, my friends. What do you neeed?"

Jajumbee explained the plan as Zani and he would go below for a time. Then he faced Boofo, gave him a hearty hug, and said, "And you, my faithful friend, will be our eyes and ears here above while we're gone."

Boofo nodded his agreement.

But Emilio said, "Eyes? Oh yes. But ears?" He raised his eyes toward the enormous ears on his own head. "Maybe mee for that."

Everyone chuckled. It was good to laugh before they parted. Who knew what future lay ahead for the Island? But maybe, just maybe, Zani and Jajumbee would find out something down below—something that could bring the Island back together again.

16

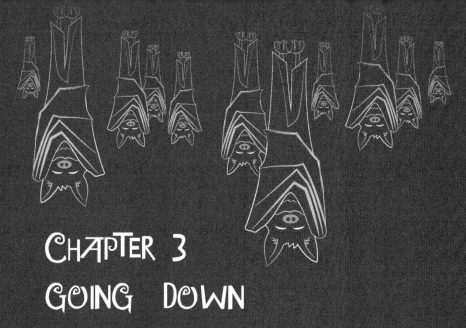

CHAPTER 3
GOING DOWN

Zani, being a sea turtle, wasn't fond of climbing up or down trees. But with Jajumbee's sticky feet and hands on the other side of the palm's trunk, she was able to work her way down with him. Awkward for any turtle—but not impossible. With Zani functioning as the leader of the sea creatures, and Jajumbee leader of the land creatures, they'd learned how to work together for the good of the whole Island, and no time was more important to do so than now.

Once they reached the cave floor at the base of the tree, the two began their descent into the dark chambers that encircled the Island's volcanic core.

Seeing the hundreds of bats sleeping upside-down, hanging on the ceiling, Jajumbee whispered to Zani, "I'll wait until we get further into the dark to light the torch."

"No need to wake them up," agreed Zani. She was reminded of orcas when the bats squeaked—a sound that still made her shiver.

But a lone bat circled down quietly and landed just in front of them. It was Emilio. "One last weesh for a safe journey, my friends." He encircled them in his wings and whispered, "And a warning to be careful below. Something eez amiss, stirring thee very heart of thee Island. "

"Do you think it will erupt again?" asked Jajumbee.

"I cannot say. I weesh I knew. Maybe Solo knows. Talk to heem."

"We will," Zani promised.

The bat then spread his wings and softly flew back to the crowded ceiling. The two voyagers walked on through the bat's chamber into the shadows beyond until they reached a hallway where the last bit of daylight remained. There Zani held the torch as Jajumbee struck flint and pyrite rocks together. The spark lit the sap-soaked leaves and flared into a small orange flame.

In the dim light, they searched the walls for any markings, but no, there was nothing here.

"The drawings are farther down," said Jajumbee, "near the stream." He clenched the torch as they

18

continued down the rocky hallway.

A draft stirred the flame. Jajumbee sang softly as they approached the narrows—a bridge of stone stretching over a deep chasm:

Oooooooo OOOooo OOooooooo OOoo,

Feel the cooling wind, blowing through the hall,

We stay on the path, wanting not to fall.

Think of what's ahead, not of what we dread,

Only emptiness below,

Only emptiness below.

Oooooooo OOOooo OOooooooo OOoo.

Here Jajumbee took the lead, his sticky feet on full alert, testing each step. Zani held on to the gecko's long tail. They walked in line, for they could not side by side. As the wind stirred in the open space around them, Jajumbee held the torch low. He focused on the narrow stone, always searching for the next foothold. There was nothing else.

"I wouldn't mind the deep," said Zani, "if I knew I could swim it."

"If one more step is all I know, I just put my mind to it."

Keep us on the path, help us not to fall.

Think not of what we dread, instead of what's ahead.

Their narrow steps were many, but not forever. The path widened until they could walk side by side again. Cave walls emerged from the void and encircled them once more. Zani's flipper stepped on wet rock in shadow before Jajumbee's torch circled round to see the sparkling stream flowing from a crack in the rock wall.

"Now we follow the water," Jajumbee smiled.

"I like that better," said the sea turtle.

"We should be seeing drawings on the walls any time now."

They strained their eyes in the flickering light as Jajumbee gently swayed the torch from one side toward the other. The rock was orange—striped in shifting shadows until . . .

"There!" Zani pointed her flipper. "Markings on the wall!"

Jajumbee turned his torch to examine them, squinting his eyes. "This cannot be," he stated. "Impossible!"

20

Chapter 4

Up Above

His two friends on their way below, Boofo quietly made his way through the underbrush alone. Trying to avoid any questions about where he'd been, the treefrog kept to himself. He stayed off the trails. Here the forest was thick and wet—palm leaves above blocked out most of the sky.

He heard a rustling in the trees—saw a flash of color. Some kind of bird . . . it looked like a parrot! Boofo hid himself in a patch of ferns and spied on the fowl creature.

The colorful bird muttered to himself, "Kee-raw, chee, caw," using his beak as a tool to crack a hard nut he'd plucked from the tree.

"Can it be?" Boofo asked himself, "Yes! Barnacle—the parrot pirate!" He hadn't seen that infamous bird since the whole pirate crew had boarded the *Black Widow* and fled the Island. The villains were defeated and driven out only when the creatures of land and sea united against them. Were the pirates back again? Boofo shivered at the thought. Or only their bird?

Suddenly the parrot hurled the nut to the ground. "Haaard!" He squawked, ruffling his feathers.

Boofo hardly dared to breathe. Then another bird tumbled through the leafy canopy. Somehow the second bird managed to grasp a palm in its claws. The branch snapped. Feathers flapping, the bird found a more solid perch nearer the parrot. Then he folded his wings and shook his bright red comb. It was a rooster! None other than Chanty himself!

"Caw," Barnacle greeted him. "Whart did ya bring me?"

Chanty presented him with a plump mango.

"Oh, thankee!" Barney clasped the fruit in his claw and took a bite. Juice dripping from his beak, he told the young rooster his news. "They's gone below." He clicked his beak and chuckled. "Spied 'em meeself."

Chanty clucked his approval.

Barney continued, "With them gone—it be time ta restore some arrrder ta the island!"

"What order?" asked the rooster.

"Aaaar order, ye comb-head! The order of the land over the sea! Whar birds rule the roost."

The rooster brushed his comb back in place. He assumed a royal position—head high, tail feathers cocked, and prepared to crow.

The parrot pinched him in the rooster's magnificent feathered neck.

"CAW-rooooo," the rooster choked.

"Not now," the parrot warned him. "Ye'll have plenty o' time fer crowin' later."

Chanty cleared his throat. "What's the plan, Mr.B.?"

"Don't clutter up yer little brain with that now— jest leave it ta me."

"Got it, boss."

"Lookee here, Chanty. Nobody's ta know I'm here. Ya' see?"

"Yessir."

"Not even yer mudder."

"Mudder?" Chanty cocked his head.

"Ya know, madre, mama—any of them flappin' hens."

"Oh, yessir!"

"You meet me here and I'll give yer instructions."

Chanty nodded his head, his comb shaking back into his eyes.

Barnacle rolled his eyes. "Jest remember—I'll do the thinkin', you do the crowin'. Before long, you'll be the king of this 'ere Island."

Chanty raised himself up again and gathered his breath.

The parrot pinched his neck again.

"CAW-rooooo," the rooster choked.

"Not now," Barney reminded him.

"Yessir."

In the underbrush below, barely moving a frog's leg, Boofo listened to the bird's plan.

"No good," he thought. "Gotta stop 'em."

But it was too soon to call for help. Jajumbee and Zani had barely started. They were looking for answers

24

in the cave, right? He sighed, then wondered if it was loud enough to hear. But thankfully the birds were still busy talking in the tree.

So Boofo thought to himself, "Up to me."

It was a big responsibility—bigger than cooking up a mess of mosquito mush—way bigger!

"Bigger than me?" he wondered. Then one of Jajumbee's songs came to mind:

> *Eeee-Ohh—Dig-uh-boom-bah-ay!*
> *Eeee-Ohh—Look at it my way!*
>
> *Pirates come, Pirates go,*
> *Causing trouble—everyone know.*
> *What if things turn dark and gray?*
> *Look beyond them—you find a way!*
>
> *Eeee-Ohh—Dig-uh-boom-bah-ay!*

Chapter 5

The Writing on the Wall

"**W**hat's the matter, Jajumbee?" asked Zani. The flickering torchlight animated the drawings surrounding them on the cave walls.

"The drawings are events—even things that just happened here on the Island . . ."

"Someone is recording our history?"

Jajumbee nodded, "Very recent history! Look at that picture of the volcano."

Zani moved closer and peered at the rocky cone—the torch made it look like the lava was still flowing—but it was the face! Her mouth dropped open as she turned to the gecko.

"It's me, right?" Jajumbee raised his eyebrows. "On the face of the mountain."

"Just like what happened!" Zani nodded. "But that was only a few days ago."

"Exactly!"agreed Jajumbee. "So who's doing this? And more importantly, when did they draw it?"

"It had to be in the past few days."

"So"—Jajumbee redirected his light to the next drawing—". . . then, what about this?"

If Zani had been surprised the first time, now she could hardly believe her eyes—the face on the volcano looked like . . . "That's Barnacle! It's the parrot pirate!" She slapped her forehead with her flippers. "What does it mean, Jajumbee?"

"I'm not sure, my friend, but perhaps we haven't seen the last of that scoundrel."

"Didn't he leave on the pirate ship with the rest of them?"

"That's what we thought. The scurvy bird was last seen chasing Lily and Rose—when those two heroic hens turned the tide of battle in our favor."

"Don't count your chickens . . . out," said Zani. It had almost become a proverb on the Island.

28

"Maybe we shouldn't count that parrot out either," warned the gecko.

"But they're just drawings," said Zani hopefully.

"Maybe." Jajumbee shrugged. "But I want to know who made them and what they know!"

"And how do they know it?" added the sea turtle.

"We'd better find Solo, the cave salamander. He lives down there."

"He's blind—he doesn't even have eyes!" Zani exclaimed. "What can he know about drawings he can't even see? And anyboby could sneak right past him."

Jajumbee reminded her, "He had no trouble finding you."

Zani had to admit that. "I was rather loud."

"It's his sense of smell, my friend—that's where he far outdoes either of us."

Zani scrunched her nose and agreed.

"So let's keep going, then. And keep our eyes on the walls along the way. Who knows what other clues we might find here?"

"Good idea. In fact, I remember a picture of two mice around here somewhere—they seemed to be

29

swimming in the bay—with a pirate ship nearby. What could that mean?"

Jajumbee spread his arms. "That, my friend, is a very long story. But a good one." He smiled.

"Who are they?" asked the turtle.

"They were known as the *Mice of the Herring Bone.*"

"Can you tell me more about them?"

"Soon enough," Jajumbee promised. "But now—we need to gather all the clues we can."

So walking along the trickling stream, they turned their attention back to the cave walls. Scenes emerged in the torch's circle of orange light—as if they were turning pages in a book of stone.

When they looked at each scene long enough, objects appeared—hidden within patterns, or in the spaces between. Were those hidden objects clues?

As the walls closed in around them, Jajumbee sang a new song:

A path in water. A tale in fire,

The past below. The future— higher?

Story in pictures? Told by a liar?
How can we know? We must inquire.

The path we take by orange flame,
Leads down—from where the lava came.
But if not fire, the path may be
A gateway to the open sea.

Below, we know the answer lies.
These drawings keep it in disguise.
But secrets that they try to keep
Will all be answered in the deep.

Chapter 6
Stony Passage

Along the trickling, flickering path, more drawings emerged in the torchlight.

"It's them—the mice!" Zani pointed. "In a balloon launched by bats?"

Jajumbee laughed, "Ah, yes! Their parting moment!"

"Where did the mice go?"

"Back on their own quest," answered the gecko. "They serve a great queen in a faraway land—carried there by the *Westing Wind*."

Before Zani could ask any more questions, the walls were filled with celebration—all the Island creatures feasting, singing, and dancing. "It's like our big celebration—after the *Black Widow* left!"

But no sooner had she mentioned the pirate ship,

33

than the light shone on its likeness. It was the scene of a great battle—not just one ship, but two—side by side! The *Black Widow* with its distinctive spider flag, and the other?

"That ship," asked Zani, "Where is it from? I think I've seen that flag before."

Jajumbee wasn't surprised. "Could be," he shrugged. "Their queen has many ships on the sea."

"So many came," Zani exclaimed, "and so much happened here!"

"Oh yes," agreed Jajumbee. "If we took a map—those who know this Island spread far and wide. The sea—it is a beeeeg place!"

"And hard to know who your neighbor is."

Jajumbee couldn't help but laugh. "You've heard that before, eh?"

Zani smiled. "From the wisest of the Island."

"You flatter me, my friend! But our history is not just found in the far and wide." His arms spread—then closed in—he pointed his torch ahead. "It is also found in the deep."

Below, we know the answer lies.

These drawings keep it in disguise.

But secrets that they try to keep

May all be answered in the deep.

Where the pictures no longer decorated the walls, three great stones split the cavern hallway. The middle stone had holes like eyes looking back at them, and an open mouth—ready to speak. Jajumbee took careful note of it, but said nothing. The cave walls then opened into a domed chamber. Inside, stalactites reached stalagmites joining floor to ceiling, making columns like a web of stone.

Jajumbee's light no longer reached the the cave's edges. And they dared not venture far from the water path. But of necessity, they squeezed through stone bars that stretched up the dome. It was a silent passage as they focused on keeping the stream in sight around every obstacle they faced. It would be easy to get lost in this dark jailhouse cavern.

How long this took, neither could be sure. In the darkness, even time can hide itself.

Gradually, the flowing water underfoot spread thin and gave way to more water overhead. They'd entered a high chamber. Here dripping water returned a sense of time to the cave travelers—seconds ticking away with each drop.

The two remembered a cheerful song from their reunion in this very place long ago:

> *Pit, pit. Pit, pitter, patter.*
>
> *Go down, See what's the matter.*
>
> *In caves, in lower places,*
>
> *Look for—familiar faces.*

"Jajumbee, this is where you and Boofo found me when I couldn't find my way out!"

"How well I remember," the gecko said, smiling.

"Solo brought me this far," she recalled.

"Then we're not far from where the water fills the cave floor," Jajumbee whispered. Drops of water landed on the flame of Jajumbee's torch and hissed.

Sssssss.

He cleared his throat. "We should find Solo soon. I know he's a bit odd—are you comfortable with him?"

36

Smiling, Zani imitated the cave salamander's distintive speech, "Oh, yesssss . . ."

"Good." Jajumbee didn't smile. "Maybe he knows what's happening down here."

The ceiling drips faded as the two made their way to a descending stone staircase—each step filled with a shallow pool.

"If it's not too much trouble," began Jajumbee, "may I take a ride?"

"Yes, of course," answered Zani. "How thoughtless of me—you've given so much help already! Get on!"

"Island Rule." Jajumbee climbed atop her shell.

"Indeed!" said Zani. "First you give, and then you can take."

They slid down the stairs—one plop at a time into each pool.

Down. Down. Down. The last step plopped them into a pool where Zani's flippers no longer touched bottom. So she swam with Jajumbee who held the flaming mast above them.

They floated into a passageway of fantastic stone formations. Jajumbee swept the torch back and forth trying to see them all—rock clusters like coconuts hung from the ceiling, while stone curtains as thin as the sail of a ship clung to the cave walls.

Sssssss. A drop of water hit the torchlight. It fizzled and dimmed.

"Let the light last," Jajumbee whispered to himself.

The current swept gently toward their right. They followed the current—the *thalweg* path—into a smooth, round passageway. Here the stone seemed like polished glass—reflecting the fading torchlight.

"Looks like we've entered a lava tube," Jajumbee said.

"Lava?" Zani glanced over her shoulder at her passenger. "You mean the volcano made this?"

"Fire has given way to water."

An eerie orange glow reflected off the rippling stream. Zani hardly noticed the change in the light. Jajumbee's torch had gone out.

Now they could feel the warmth, from a hole in the curving rock wall just ahead. It was glowing hot.

"The very heart of the volcano," said Jajumbee.

Zani shuddered as she remembered how she'd swum toward that hole in the wall before—fearing the cave salamander who chased her—saving her from the fire.

Jajumbee felt her shell shake under his feet. "Are you OK, my friend?"

"I'm OK." Zani paddled over to the far side, away from the lava in the rock. She looked over her shoulder as they passed by and noticed the torch was out. Only a smouldering plume trailed behind them.

"Jajumbee! Your torch!"

To Zani's surprise, Jajumbee had a broad smile on his face. "We need it no longer!" He spread out his arms and stared ahead. "Look!"

Zani turned to see they had just drifted into a huge chamber. On the cave ceiling, hundreds, perhaps thousands, of blueish lights formed what seemed a false sky of unfamiliar constellations.

"The glow worms!" cried Zani. "Solo's chamber of lights!"

Jajumbee gazed upward, embracing the underground "sky." "What a pity Solo can't see this beauty."

"I think he tastes it," said Zani. And the two couldn't help but smile, as the dim light shifted from fire-orange to ocean blue.

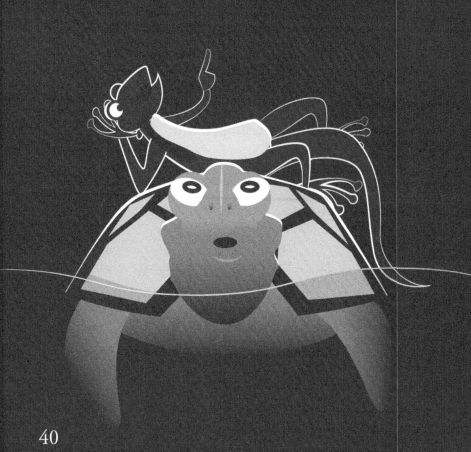

CHAPTER 7

NEW COMPANION

By now, the two friends were very hungry. Who knew how long they'd been underground? Hours? Or days? They munched their snacks as they drifted through the sparkling reflection of the glow worms. Jajumbee lay face up on Zani's shell. He made up new constellations from the patterns above.

"I see a bigger dipper!" he declared. "And it's full of Blessing Stew!"

Zani laughed. "How about that cluster there?"

"Hmmm," the gecko thought, "I think it's a heroic sea turtle."

"Oh really?"

"The great constellation Panzanilla!"

"Me?"

"Of course."

"And is there a heroic gecko?"

"Perhaps." Jajumbee pointed to a corner of the cave. "Maybe those dim 'stars' over yonder."

One fell and plopped into the water.

"Oops! Looks like you dropped something." Zani smiled.

"Not a problem. As long as the turtle stays strong." Jajumbee took a bite of the food they'd brought along for the trip.

"Um, do these constellations have stories, too?"

"Of course," Jajumbee replied, still munching, "but their songs are still being written."

"A song—of course!" Zani smiled. "So, will you sing one?"

He took his last bite of mango, and agreed to try:

Ummm-hmmm, Ummm-hmmm-hmmm

In the land of all night,
Shine the stars of this song.
Up above is the fright!
For a hero they long.
There's a face on the mount,
But it doesn't belong.

Panzanilla the great,
She holds our Island's fate.
In the deep lies the sea,
And that's no place for me.

Ooooo-noo, Ooooo-noo,

The Island exploded,
From the ocean below.
Fire came from the water,
Where the sea turtles go.

43

"Now just a minute!" Zani interrupted him, "What do you mean? You're not going?"

"I'm not. I can't go, Zani. I'm a freshwater gecko—I'm not fit for those salty deep waters. I brought you this far. Now it's Solo's turn to guide you. We can only hope he knows the way."

Zani closed her eyes and shook her head. "No! I'm not going then!"

Jajumbee leaned down to hug her neck and whispered, "You can take this journey, Zani. If we are to know what's to happen on the Island, the answer could be hidden deep in its history—mined by one who knows the very heart of the volcano—the artist who made the cave drawings. Then he, or she, filled them with hidden clues."

Zani turned to him and asked, "Are you sure the artist is there? The one who knows the answers?"

"I cannot be sure," answered Jajumbee, "but why would the volcano call me?"

"You mean the face—your face—on the mountain . . . it really was a message?"

"Maybe I was called to read the cave drawings."

"Do you know what they mean?"

"Not completely, but the drawings did point to an answer."

"What answer?"

"Remember the rock with the face—the turtle's face—that opened into a dome—a dome shaped chamber like the inside of a turtle shell . . ."

"Wait! What?" Zani's eyes opened wide, "So we walked through a turtle shell?"

Jajumbee nodded. "In stone . . . it was almost as if a turtle had spoken those drawings."

"But you were the one telling me what they meant!"

"And now I'm telling you that the key to understanding the clues we saw, could be a turtle."

Their moment of silence was interrupted by the sound of ripples approaching, formed by the wake of a long white tail. It was swimming over from where they saw the glow worm fall.

An eyeless white head popped above the surface, then opened its mouth in a wide, glowing grin. It squealed with delight, "My friendsssssss!"

CHAPTER 8

BACK TO BOOFO

Nestled back in his tree by the forest stream, Boofo paid close attention to the buzz of more than just the mosquitoes around him. There was a stir among the Island creatures, a disturbing turn of attitude, a growing division between land and sea.

He overheard two tiny green lizards talking in the grass.

"Did you hear Chanty's latest cackle?" asked the first.

"Sure did," answered the second. "He's got a great point!"

Boofo couldn't help but think of the lizard's choice of words. "Lots of points—beak, claws. Better watch out!" he thought to himself.

The two reptiles continued talking.

"Of course the sea creatures don't care if the volcano blows sky high." The lizard threw his hands up. "They can just escape into the ocean!"

"And what about us?" the other nodded. "They'll leave us behind to be covered in ash!"

"Right!" The first lizard spread his arms. "Why should we trust them?"

The second flicked his tongue and shook his head. "I sure don't!"

"Me neither! I'm with Chanty on that!"

"Me too!"

A distant rooster crow echoed through the forest. Boofo couldn't help but roll his eyes.

The two lizards hurried off in that direction.

Jajumbee and Zani had left just over a day ago, and it seemed like Barnacle's plan was already working. The Island creatures had forgotten so quickly!

The sea creatures helped save the Island from pirates. Torpedo the dolphin and his friends were heroes. And what about Zani? The Island would be ruled by pirate seadogs now if it weren't for her!

Boofo decided to hop after those two lizards and set them straight. He plopped into the soft grass, and caught up with them in just a few jumps.

"Hey!" he croaked.

The startled lizards scrambled up a fern for cover.

"No harm," said Boofo. "Just talk."

The lizards peered down at him through the fronds.

"Heard you talking," Boofo said. "Not right!"

The lizards looked at each other—frowning at the very thought of being corrected by an amphibian.

But the treefrog continued, "No trust Chanty."

"What do you know?" asked the first lizard. "Did you listen to his cackle?"

"No," Boofo answered. "Crows too much."

"Wait a minute," the second lizard narrowed his eyes. "You're Jajumbee's friend, aren't you? The gecko that's always singing his rules."

"Island Rule!" Boofo corrected him.

Nobody break-a thee Island Rule!

"Hah!" the first lizard scoffed, "What good are his rules when the Island is about to blow up?"

"And just who does Jajumbee think he is—putting his face on the volcano like that?" the other lizard gestured toward the mountain face.

"Isn't the gecko a friend of that sea turtle too?" asked the first lizard.

Boofo nodded. "Zani."

"A sea creature . . ." sneered the same lizard.

"Chanty warned us about them," added the second. "He's watching out for us—the Island creatures."

"No—not Chanty," Boofo warned them. "His friend is pirate!"

The lizards just laughed at him.

"Ha, ha, hee, hee! Where did you hear that nonsense, treefrog?" asked one.

"From Chanty."

They laughed again.

One lizard grabbed ahold of his tail, and waved

it like a sword toward the other. "Maybe we are all pirates!" he chuckled. "Yo, ho ho!"

The other lizard grabbed his tail too, and they pretended a sword fight there on the fern.

Boofo hung his head and turned a brighter shade of orange.

The rooster's call in the distance jerked the lizards out of their swordplay.

"Let's go!" said the first lizard. "Everyone will be there!"

"To hear what we all know is *really* happening on the Island!" agreed the second. "From Chanty!"

"Goodbye, treefrog!" They scampered away, snickering at Boofo.

"New rules," Boofo muttered to himself. "Pirate-made rules."

But the lizards didn't hear him.

So Boofo decided it was time to call Emilio out from the cave. If anyone would listen, he would.

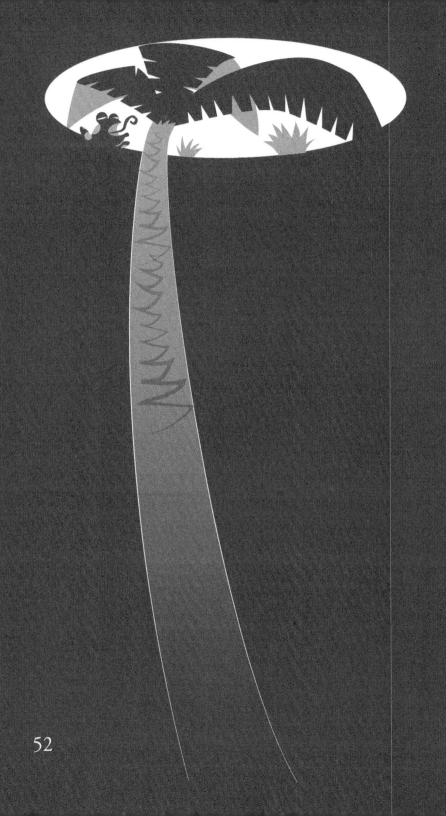

CHAPTER 9
CALLING ALL BATS

It was late afternoon by the time Boofo arrived back at the Short Tree entrance to the caves. Every twilight the bats rushed out into the night like a cloud. So he needed to get Emilio's attention soon. Boofo cleared his throat—stretching it out like a bubble, then deflating it again, until he was ready. He closed his eyes and leaned just over the edge of the dark cave entrance.

"Squeeeeee . . . ." his croak rose higher and higher in pitch until only the best of ears could hear.

Boofo waited, peering into the dark, until a lone gray bat flew up to greet him at the mouth of the cave.

"You called mee?"

Boofo nodded. "Trouble."

"What eez it?"

"Chanty . . . and Barnacle," the treefrog croaked.

Alarmed, Emilio sat patiently as Boofo told his story syllable by syllable. The treefrog ended his story with a simple question. "What now?"

The bat scratched his furry head, trying to think of an answer.

"Forgetful," said Boofo.

"I'm sorry, Boofo, Eet's not that I've forgotten. I just don't know."

Boofo shook his head. "Not you—Island creatures —they forget history."

Understanding now, Emilio nodded, then asked, "How many? How many have forgotten?"

Boofo shrugged, "Not sure. Heard of many. But only two . . ." He held up his hands.

"Two ears?" Emilio spread his wings in excitement. "Yes, we need more ears!"

"Lizards," Boofo muttered, but then he got it. "Yes! More ears. Two not enough."

"We have plenty of ears." Emilio smiled. "And good ones, too! I'll tell the bats to listen carefully tonight by

54

thee campfires"—he swooped one wing—"by dens and nests and hollows!" He swooped his other wing. "Then they'll report to mee in the cave tomorrow morning."

"Good plan." Boofo nodded.

"Then wee'll know how far this pirate poison has spread by Chanty's crowing of catastrophe! Perhaps eet's not too late to turn thee tide!"

"Bring Island back together," Boofo croaked hopefully.

"Oh yes, my friend," agreed Emilio. "The creatures could get so fearful of thee Island blowing up—that they may blow it up themselves first!"

"By Chanty's words," Boofo agreed.

"Barnacle's words een disguise," added Emilio.

Then the bat spread his wings and turned toward the cave. But he looked over his shoulder at Boofo and said, "Get on my back. Come, tell thee bats your story."

The treefrog ducked his head. There were hundreds, maybe thousands of bats in the cave. How could he speak, er, croak to so many?

Emilio saw it and said, "Do not fear, Boofo. They will hear you."

As fearful as he felt of speaking to a cavern full of bats, Boofo knew he must. So he climbed onto Emilio's back and gripped the bat's fur until it pinched him.

"Ready," he croaked.

Emilio smiled and nodded. "The tide eeez turning already, my friend. Fear itself trembles at your courage."

At that, Boofo raised his head up, and Emilio launched back into the deep, singing:

Bat in thee cave, an' fish in thee school

—Nobody break-a thee Island Rule!

Frogs hopping 'round on mo-skee-to fuel

—Nobody break-a thee Island Rule!

CHAPTER 10

PARTING WAYS

In the cave's dim light, Solo's glowing grin was a welcome sight, especially with Jajumbee's torch out. But what could the blind cave salamander know of the recent stirrings in the volcano, or of its history?

"Jajumbee and Zani—if my nose does not de-ssss-ceive me." Solo greeted them, "Ssso good of you to return! But where'ssss my cousin, Boofo?"

"Boofo's on duty up above," answered Jajumbee, "But he sends his regards."

"Likewisssse," said Solo, his long tail swishing back and forth in the dark water. "But tell me—what bringsss you?"

Jajumbee got to the point. "You know there are drawings on the walls of the cave, right?"

"Yessss, I know them. Though . . . I think of them as carvings."

"So they are," agreed the gecko. "And . . . do you know who put them there?"

"The artist?" Solo scratched his chin. "Hmmm. All I can ssssay is that those sstories come from the deep. Sssomething that sssmells of the sssalt of the sssea brought them here."

Zani looked at Jajumbee. Somehow he'd known this quest must go deeper than a gecko could go.

"We need your help," said Zani, then restated, ". . . rather, *I* need your help."

"You are going to the deep," Solo guessed.

"Do you know the way?" asked Zani.

"I know of a gateway," answered the salamander, adding, "underwater."

Zani looked at Jajumbee. "You knew I had to go without you, didn't you?"

"Remember, my friend, the cave drawings, they pointed to a turtle. I cannot dive into the salty waters.

Only you can venture into the deep, Zani."

The sea turtle considered his words. "Solo, how far can you take me?" she asked.

"To the sssalting of the waters," answered Solo.

Zani cocked her head. "Which is . . . ?"

"Where ssseawater divides itss-self from fresh," said Solo.

"The *halocline*." Jajumbee nodded.

"How do you know of this?"asked Zani.

"By my friends from the sea," Jajumbee smiled. "It's good to learn more than only what one can experience himself."

"Ssso true," agreed Solo. "By such means even I have sseen the ssstars."

Zani looked up at the glow worms Jajumbee had named after her—the great "constellation" Panzanilla. "Do any of them represent a turtle?" she asked, with a wink toward Jajumbee.

She was surprised to hear Solo's answer. "Only in the most ancient ssstories. Three ssstars in a line represented the turtle's shell—but now, it is mossstly known as Orion's Belt."

"Really? Orion's Belt was a turtle?" Zani could hardly believe it. "Seriously?"

"Ssssseriously."

Even Jajumbee seemed surprised. "The ancients understood the importance of turtles."

"There are many sssecretsss in the deep. The layers of time are sswept away in passsageways of ssalt and ssstone."

Zani was beginning to think this quest might reveal more than she was expecting.

"So then," said Jajumbee, "it's time I must be going. But I have two requests of you, Solo."

"You need only asssk."

"First, something for my torch to light the return."

Solo gave him a glowing grin, and said, "I know jussst the thing." He stuck the torch in his mouth to cover it in glowing goop. "But your sssecond request issss . . . ?"

"Keep her safe to the gateway of the salt sea." And Jajumbee gave Zani a hug. Then she dropped the gecko off on the stony shore and waved a flipper toward her friend. He returned a wave with his blue-glowing torch.

"Jajumbee, sing us a song," Zani called.

Hooo-oooo. She follow the water,
Hooo-ooo. That's where we got her.

Down deep, in lower places,
We'll miss—familiar faces.

A salty tear spilled from the corner of Zani's eye. Just a taste of what lay further down below.

CHAPTER 11

GOING SOLO

Zani and Solo watched as Jajumbee's blue torch flickered against the cavern walls. She hadn't considered how alone the gecko would be until that moment, only her own lonely quest.

"Ssssoo," asked the salamander, "how long can you hold it?"

"Not sure what you mean."

"Your breath," he continued. "I've got gills mysssself."

"A few hours I suppose." Zani shrugged. "I've never bothered to keep time."

"We don't keep time much down here, either," said Solo, "but there are only a few places to find air where we're going—you can't jussst go to the sssurface wherever you want."

"I suppose not."

"Once we get to the gateway, you'll find sssome air pocketsss . . . along the ceilings."

Zani wondered out loud, "Ceilings?"

"Yes, in the ancient ssstructures."

"You mean, there are buildings down below?"

"Oh yessss, you'll sssseee."

Apparently there was more below than she could have imagined! So she took her deepest breath, and the two of them dove under the surface of the water. Soon the "starry" ceiling faded away. Zani kept an eye on Solo's glowing mouth.

"Stay close," Zani requested. "I can't see much."

"Of course!" Solo exclaimed. Then he plucked a fallen glow worm out of the water and handed it to her. "Smear some on your flippers," he suggested.

It seemed rather goopy and gross—but it did help light her way in the deep.

"Sssoon the water will be clear."

She hoped he was right about that. Now, all she could see was grains of sand suspended, drifting slowly in the water.

"How far?"

"You'll know when we reach the sssalty layer. Of course, I'm not made for the sssea—after we reach sssalt, you'll have to sswim on alone."

Zani knew this was her quest, but when Solo said it so clearly, it sent a shiver down her shell.

She focused only on keeping Solo in her sight until she noticed another surface there under the surface— they'd reached a rippling layer—like a painting in progress.

"Almossst there!" Solo announced. As they swam under the halocline layer, the water suddenly cleared. Of course, it was still dark—no sunbeams reached this depth. However, what little light they had, was more useful, as if they had suddenly emerged from a fog.

"Wow!" said Zani, "What a quick change!"

"For me, too, I cannot ssstay," said Solo. He swung around to face Zani and pointed toward a stone structure in the distance. "Ssstraight ahead," he told her, "the gateway."

Zani squinted in the dim light—yes that must be it.

"Besssst of luck!" said the salamander. Then with a flip of his tail, he passed through the salt barrier, back into the fresh water above, and out of sight.

Zani refocused on the stone blocks ahead and paddled alone toward the gateway. It was farther than she thought. "Those blocks must be huge!"

After a long swim, she finally passed through the giant gateway. She felt so small! The stone blocks surely weighed tons. That must have been why they were still standing after so long. Only the ancients could have built something like this. And why, wondered Zani, had it been built underwater? But wait, if had been built underwater, there would be no air pockets, and she couldn't hold her breath forever!

But Solo had told her to look to the ceiling, so Zani did. She heard a gurgling noise—the sound of air! Paddling upward she broke the water's surface and took a deep breath. It sent her into a coughing fit.

"Eww, so stale!" she thought. "Guess I'd better get used to it."

Zani found herself inside a dome cut from a massive single stone. Carvings covered the ceiling— intricate swirls and geometric shapes within large tiles. "It almost looks like I'm inside a huge turtle shell!" she said to herself.

She took another deep breath and dove back into

the entry hall again. More carvings on the walls! She wished Jajumbee was here to help her figure out what they meant. Or just to make sure she was going the right way. It reminded her of the song they'd sung passing over the stone bridge at the Narrows.

Ooooooo OOOooo OOoooooo OOoo,

Feel the rolling tide, pulling through the stone,

Keep me on the path, even all alone.

Think of what's ahead, not of what I dread,

Only emptiness below,

Only emptiness below.

Ooooooo OOOooo OOoooooo OOoo.

But what was ahead? Zani would only know when she got there. Maybe she'd find some answers.

CHAPTER 12

JAJUMBEE'S ASCENT

Jajumbee considered his options. He was so close to the other cave entrance, but that was practically straight up the rocks. And those rocks were often slippery, especially when a waterfall spilled from the rains in the forest above. It was dry now. Was it worth the chance? He was a gecko after all—with sticky pads on his feet.

"Why not?" So he worked his way around the shoreline of Solo's lake under the light of the cavern chamber's glow worm "stars." When he got to the place where the waterfall-bed path led up to the surface, he squinted his eyes and peered upward. He couldn't see any daylight. Maybe the path curved around too much? Or maybe it was just nighttime? It was hard to keep track of time down in the caves.

69

There was no rope, no steps—and he couldn't tell how far to the surface. He'd have to rock-climb the whole way up. Couldn't carry the torch that way. But here, there were the glow worms, and by the time he got higher surely there would be at least a bit of daylight, or moonlight, coming in.

No more second-guessing! Jajumbee started up the steep path, just hoping it wouldn't rain.

It seemed pretty easy at first. He looked back over his shoulder to check his progress. Not bad—and a nice view, too. The dark lake reflected the glow worms on the ceiling so they looked like twinkling stars. But enough of that—he was going up to see the real ones in the night sky.

Step by step, further and further up until he was level with the cave ceiling itself. He could see the glow worms hanging down from the rocks. So many! But not so enchanting when they were close by. Jajumbee even wondered, "If Solo could see the worms, would he still eat them?"

Continuing upward, the gecko entered into a dark rocky shaft. Here the waterfall-bed was no longer dry. A trickling stream of water bounced back and forth between rocks along the way, breaking into drips that each found their own way into the cave.

Jajumbee looked back over his shoulder again—but maybe he shouldn't have. It was a looong way down. "I don't want to follow the water here—that's for sure!"

A flash from above lit the passageway.

"What was that?"

But too soon Jajumbee had his answer, as the roll of thunder echoed down from above.

"Ooooh-noooo! Bad time for a rainstorm—the worst!"

He was nearly out of breath from his climb already, and it was so hard to see!

Another flash—and Jajumbee used the light to scope out his best path forward. There was a ledge not far above. He pulled himself up another few steps. He reached into the blackness, but couldn't find a handhold. So he waited.

The trickling stream was growing. He could even feel some splashing beside him.

"Ooooh—not good!"

Another lightning flash—and Jajumbee saw his way to the safety of the ledge. He tucked himself against the wall as thunder crashed in the sky beyond. Then came the downpour.

Water gushed down the walls now. It even flowed like a curtain right in front of his little ledge.

"No climbing now!" He kept his feet stuck to the rocks and pulled his tail in between his legs. "Just stick around," he sighed hopefully.

Then he thought he heard a voice.

"Jajumbee?"

"I'm up here!" shouted the gecko, hoping to be heard above the noise of the waterfall.

Up here, came back his echo.

"Jajumbee? Are you sssafe?" asked Solo.

You sssafe? came the echo.

It was Solo!

"I sssaw your torch," the salamander said.

Your torch.

"Yes! It's me, Jajumbee!"

"Sssstay where you are!"

You are.

Another flash of lightning.

"Oooh, I will!"

I will.

"I will . . ."

Booo-RUUM-Bah! Thunder interrupted Solo's answer. Or was it just another echo?

With the water pouring down in front of him, Jajumbee pressed himself into the rock ledge. There was nothing more he could do . . . except sing:

> *Goes down, down goes the water,*
>
> *In caves, in lower places,*
>
> *Look for—familiar faces.*

CHAPTER 13

BAT NEWS

Boofo's eyes were either wide open or tight shut the whole way as Emilio dodged around trees of the forest, then around stalactites as they entered the cave's Bat's Door. Boofo held tight onto the fur of Emilio's back the entire flight. At last the bat folded his wings, and they both hung from the cave's ceiling.

"Are you OK?" asked Emilio.

Feeling like his belly was in his throat, Boofo croaked, "Up is down."

"My apologeees!" the bat shook his head and spread his wings again. He dropped off the ceiling, glided to a ledge along the cave wall, and placed Boofo there, right-side-up.

"Better?"

Boofo nodded, rubbed his jelly belly, and spread his feet for better balance.

Wings still unfolded, Emilio stood on the ledge facing him. "Let meee tell the group that you have an important story—and a job for them tonight."

"Um, OK." The treefrog gulped.

Then Emilio folded his wings as if he were drawing back a curtain—and Boofo was on stage!

Hundreds of bats turned their faces towards them, as Emilio began. "Wee have a guest here tonight. Some of you may know Boofo the treeefrog." He gestured toward the wide-eyed frog. "It seems a poison eez spreading on the Island—a poison of deevision. Tell them what you saw and heard, Boofo."

"Um, OK." He cleared his throat, and it squeaked, "Like he said." Boofo cleared his throat again. "Some-one dividing us." He paused. And all the bats waited. " . . . Barnacle."

There were gasps and high-pitched squeals through-out the chamber.

"The pirate. I know," Boofo nodded, "We thought . . . he went."

Many bats nodded.

"But no. He fills . . . Chanty's head . . . with lies."

Boofo gulped.

"Says . . . *no* to sea creatures . . . not to trust them."

The bats looked shocked at such a concept.

Boofo continued, "Chanty crows . . . so much. How many listen? Some do. But . . . many?" He shrugged.

The treefrog started to point to his own "ears," but instead pointed to Emilio's ears. "Your ears better!"

Several bats nodded. That was obvious!

"Listen tonight!" he asked of them. "Do many . . . trust Chanty? Do many . . . not trust . . . sea creatures? Listen!"

Boofo blinked, gazing at the crowd of bats who'd literally hung on his every word.

Finally he said, "That's all."

Emilio turned and thanked him for the report. The bats unfolded their wings and flapped them in applause for Boofo. Some even saluted, committing to listen as requested.

The flapping got even louder as the bats began their exit from the cave. They squeaked and flitted out around the Short Tree, out the Bat's Door, and into the blue-ing twilight.

Boofo cleared his throat—it squeaked too.

"Excellent speeech, my friend," said Emilio, "couldn't have said eet better myself!"

Boofo shuffled on the ledge and felt his orange grow brighter.

"Now, would you fly with meee again? I theeenk we should find Jajumbee, and tell heeem what eez happening."

"Into cave?"

"He eez there, right?"

Boofo nodded.

"Let's go." Emilio offered his furry back for Boofo to sit on once again.

Boofo took a deep breath, hopped on, and got a good grip. "Let's go!"

So off they flew into the darkness of the cavern. There was no need for Boofo to close his eyes here. Bat radar guided their path as Emilio flitted right and left, up and down—dodging obstacles that neither could see. All Boofo could do was hang on tight and trust his friend's big ears.

They passed through narrow paths where echoes bounced back quickly, and chambers where the echoes took longer. They heard a trickling stream. They felt the pitter patter of water drops from the ceiling. More splashing, like pools of water . . . and then a voice!

"Whoever it is, come help ussss!"

"Solo?" croaked Boofo.

"Cousin Boofo!" replied the cave salamander, "Thankss sso much for coming! Jajumbee needs sssome help!"

"I'm heere," replied Emilio.

"Even better!" said Solo. "The waterfall . . . high on the waterfall!"

"Jajumbee eez there?"

"Yes!"

"Uh-oh!"

"Yessss!" agreed Solo. "Go ahead! I'll come as fassst as I can behind you."

"Hold on, Boofo!" said Emilio, flying faster, his radar squeaking in rapid fire.

Soon they'd reached the great chamber of the glow worms. On its far side, the waterfall crashed down to the rocks. By now the storm had mostly passed, but the waterflow from above kept coming.

The bat fluttered to a stop in mid-air just in front of the thundering curtain of water.

"Up high!" Boofo reminded him. Up they flew.

"Jajumbee!" croaked Boofo.

"Jajumbeeee!" Emilio called. Then the bat twitched one of his huge ears. "I hear him!"

Flying up along the edge of the falls, even Boofo could hear him now.

"I am here!"

Here, came the echo.

They flew into the dark shaft. A flash of lightning revealed a tail—a gecko's tail—waving from a rocky ledge, poking through the stream of water.

"There!" shouted Boofo, leaning forward to point past Emilio's nose.

"I see heeem!"

Then Boofo climbed from Emilio's back and wrapped himself into the bat's toes. "Hold tight!"

The bat did. Fluttering in place, toes extended

toward the stream of water, Emilio positioned himself as best he could without allowing the water to cover his wings and send them tumbling.

Next it was up to Boofo. Wrapped around the bat's toes, the frog pushed his head through the falls. Water pelted his face. He couldn't even keep his eyes open. But the treefrog reached out his arms . . . and felt two arms reach back to grasp his own.

"Let's go!" croaked Boofo, the water beating at his face. "Now!"

"Ready!" shouted Jajumbee, and he was pulled through the falls in Boofo's grasp.

The two dangled down, swinging from Emilo's toes.

The bat flapped away from the falling water, then began a gentle spiral down toward the water below. Glow worm "stars" twinkled in the ever-circling ripples where the falls joined the cavern pool. A larger glow swam by them. It was the grinning salamander.

"Ex-sssell-lent ressscue!" exclaimed Solo. "Mossssst excellent! I could sssmell the excitement!"

The other three laughed and had to agree.

"Maybeee," smiled Emilo, "we should go out thee other way?"

"An ex-sell-lent idea!" Jajumbee agreed. Then remembered, asking, "And our friend, Panzanilla?"

Solo nodded, "She's on her own, down below."

"As it must be," said the gecko. "She has her task, and we have ours."

Boofo nodded, "Ours . . . maybe bigger."

"Yes, my friends, we'd best beee going back," said Emilio.

Jajumbee cocked his head with a worried look on his face.

"Come," croaked Boofo. "Hear the bats."

"I will hear them," answered Jajumbee. "And thank you for helping me—all of you!"

So Boofo and Jajumbee climbed onto Emilio's furry back and got a good hold. They bade Solo goodbye. The bat flapped past the glow-worm-covered ceiling. Jajumbee looked toward the constellation Panzanilla— the three stars in a row. Perhaps it was a hopeful sign.

CHAPTER 14

OUT OF SIGHT

The wide underwater hallway Zani had entered was made of cut stones They were so big to be lifted into place—yet they fit snugly together like puzzle pieces. Zani's eyes had adjusted to the darkness, with only the dim light from her glowing fins. So she looked for any kind of clue, something about the Island, its history. Perhaps some inkling of the Island's future was hidden here.

Then she wondered, what if the ancients built this structure before the volcano had even risen from the sea? What if . . . what if it was built on the seashore before the sea rose to its present level? That had to be it! That meant where she was floating right now was older than the volcano, older than the Island itself! Yes, this was deep time—beyond the familiar timekeepers of day and night.

"Did the volcano destroy the ancients?" Zani asked herself. "But this building—it's still here. And if this place survived the rise of the sea, and the raising of a fiery island mountain—could someone, something inside it, survive too? Maybe the artist?" An intriguing thought, but was it even possible?

The puzzled-pieced walls eventually gave way to even larger stones—megaliths—carved with intricate indecipherable designs. She swam along one side of the hallway, admiring the carvings that seemed to cover the walls from the bottom up to where the structure faded into darkness.

"Wow!" she exclaimed, a few bubbles escaping her mouth. A school of tiny fish swam past her. Perhaps they were curious. Zani noticed that their kind looked familiar. They weren't from the cave—they were from the sea—maybe the reef along the shore? So it couldn't be too far away. Maybe other, larger creatures of the reef also ventured here?

Zani paddled up into the dark to see where the wall carvings ended. Up, up, up. "These wall stones must weigh tons!" she thought. "Perhaps they could survive a volcano." Eventually she reached the ceiling. It was still intact—no exit into the ocean beyond. And she found more carvings.

She realized some were pictures of animals she'd never seen before. Large, powerful-looking land animals—bigger than any on the Island today. Yes, the ancient world had been very different from the present. But one animal was common to both times and Zani recognized it easily. It was a sea turtle.

"Looks like turtles were here before the Island was!" Zani considered that carefully, and she thought it would be useful if the creatures of the Island were aware of that history. After all, it was their history too. Sea turtles were hardly strangers to the Island shores.

Pushed gently along in the slow incoming tide, Zani floated forward. Pictures faded in and out of the dim glowing light. She felt she was in a dream, drifting back in time. In fact, it was so peaceful Zani closed her eyes and fell asleep.

Suddenly, she felt a powerful push of water— much too close. The force twirled her around. In the dim light, Zani glimpsed a white fin, a huge white fin! All she could think of was a shark! It must have followed the fish from the reef. She tried to hide her glowing fins so she could blend into the dark waters. But she knew a shark was not known for its vision, but for its keen sense of smell. She had to find a place to hide!

Zani scrambled along the wall—looking for some hole or any other safe spot. But it was so dark she could only see a paddle's length ahead of her. The walls were solid—no missing puzzle pieces.

Then she realized that all her scrambling—her panic—was using up her breath. She had to find an air pocket!

Sounds of gurgling water echoed above her again. Air! Zani paddled up into another stone dome bigger than before. She broke the surface and gasped, thankful the air wasn't stale. Instead it smelled of salt, like the smell given off by creatures that dwell in the sea. Once her head cleared, Zani realized she could see because, there was light—something was glowing up here! A greenish glow lit the water's surface.

Was this dome another giant stone turtle shell? It was tiled like one. Zani studied the ceiling to see if there were three stars in a row like in the ancient turtle constellation. Yes! Some of those shapes looked to be stars. Was this place really older than Orion and his famous belt? As old as the turtle constellation of the ancient night sky?

Slowly, Zani turned, peering around the dome's edge. She sniffed the air again. Was something in here? It sure smelled like it! She saw there was a lip of stone around the rim. Maybe a place to hide? Zani paddled toward it. But before she could reach the edge, something approached from below. White, with fins that reflected the glowing light. But it was no shark—it looked more like an underwater moon. Matching the big dome's shape, the creature was was rising up, and would fill it. Zani had no place to go!

A stream of bubbles lapped at her tail. Then Zani felt herself being lifted up out of the water. The "moon" was actually a massive white shell. It broke the surface, and water spilled off in all directions. Zani spilled off too—off the creature's back, tumbling into the water.

Wide-eyed, Zani shook the water from her face and blinked. Then blinked again. Before her floated a huge white sea turtle looking her right in the eye. Just the eye was nearly as big as Zani herself!

The great eye squinted, and the pale turtle turned its head toward her. "Why have you come?"

Zani stuttered, "I . . . I, I was sent."

"For what purpose, Little One?"

"I am called Panzanilla,"she announced, "and I've come to find answers in the deep."

That made the giant sea turtle smile, wrinkling her

face so it looked like coral. "You may call me Abuela."

"Abuela," Zani repeated. "That's a beautiful name! What does it mean?"

"Oh, it's more than a name," smiled the pale turtle. "It means *grandmother*."

CHAPTER 15

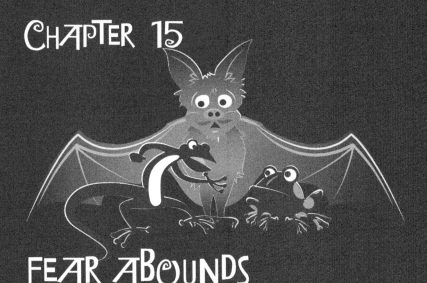

FEAR ABOUNDS

Squeaking chatter echoed from the cavern walls. There was so much noise, the bats barely noticed as Emilio returned with Jajumbee and Boofo riding on his back.

Emilio spread his wings to silence the crowd. "Sounds like you have stories to tell!" he said.

"Oh, my goodness," one bat started, "so many listen to Chanty!"

"And Chanty listens to Barnacle," Boofo added.

Another bat groaned, "It's like they theenk they can have an island without thee seeea!"

Jajumbee rolled his eyes at the news.

"And they don't trust you eeeither, Jajumbee!" said another bat, "You want to know thee reeason? Because you are a friend of thee sea turtle, Zaneee! They say no one from the seeea can be trusted. They will all abandon us."

"And your face on the rocks of the volcano!" squeaked another. "They say eetz a warning —to stay away from you!"

"It may be safer for you to stay heeeere," Emilio offered, "for you, too, Boofo."

The gecko and treefrog looked at each other, wondering what to do next.

"Are they afraid the volcano will blow up again?" asked Jajumbee. "Is that the problem?"

"Oh yeees!" several bats agreed.

"Eeetz all they talk about!" added one.

"Those creatures have lived next to that volcano their whole lives!" Jajumbee spread his hands and shook his head.

"Fear it now," said Boofo.

"Because Chanty is always crowing an alarm like the sky is falling," said Jajumbee.

Boofo scrunched his face. "Volcano skies . . . they fall."

"OK, bad example," Jajumbee admitted. "What I mean to say is that Chanty is acting like this is some *new* danger—something we've never faced before."

"And hee's using it to blame somebody," added Emilio, "our friends from thee seeea!"

Jajumbee nodded. "And me."

"Me too," croaked Boofo.

"So, anybody hear their plan?" asked Jajumbee. "What will they do?"

"New rules!" squeaked one bat. "Chanty will decide them."

"Hee will keep thee Island safe, hee says," added another. "His crows will bee our new songs."

If Jajumbee wasn't upset already, that was like a slap in the face. "So the songs we have always been singing—they are not good enough anymore?"

"I guess not, Jajumbee," Emilio said. "They want Chanty's songs now."

"Barnacle's songs," croaked Boofo, "pirate songs."

At that thought, a great sadness came over the

whole group. Then Boofo opened his mouth and made a croak that changed everything.

"Not us," declared the treefrog. "We sing Jajumbee's songs!" And to everyone's surprise, the frog began singing:

> *Oh-OHH-oh! Dig-uh-boom-bah-ay!*
>
> *That bird, crowin' to start day,*
>
> *Cries "jump"—they ask him "which way?"*
>
> *Who says, "listen what he say?"*
>
> *We know just livin' by rules,*
>
> *Leaves us just playin' the fools!*
>
> *It's deeper—comes from the heart,*
>
> *A keeper—the way that's smart!*
>
> *Our songs, bring us together,*
>
> *On land, or in the water.*
>
> *Dig, dig, dig-uh-boom-bah-aaaaay!*
>
> *Dig, dig, dig-uh-boom-bah-aaaaay!*

When Boofo had finished, he took a deep breath, and he looked bigger than ever.

Jajumbee smiled. "Thank you, my friend! But these songs—they are not just *my* songs—they belong to all of us. What we sing are the songs of the Island."

"And," added Boofo, "of sea."

Everyone agreed, and the entire cavern of bats lifted their voices to sing the song together with Boofo and Jajumbee.

"The whole Island will sing this together one day," said Emilio, "while Chanty crows alone."

"I hope you're right," said Jajumbee, "but we need a story more powerful than Chanty's . . ."

"And Barnacle's," added Boofo.

"Yes, more powerful than their divisive fables," agreed Jajumbee. "We need to tell them the story that is true!"

Boofo leaned toward his friend and said, "Maybe from below."

"Yes—when Zani returns from the deep."

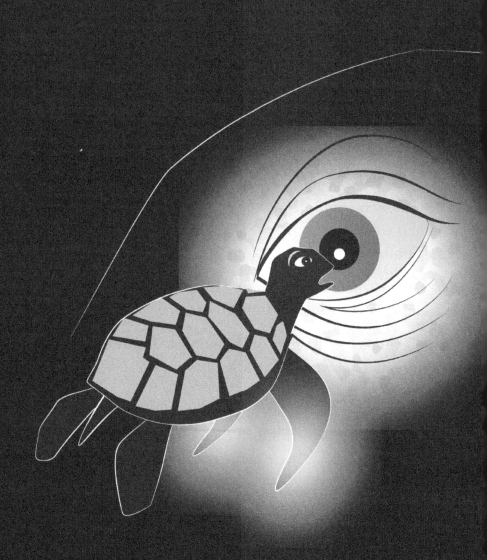

CHAPTER 16

TALES OF ABUELA

"My grandmother?" Zani wondered, could it possibly be true?

"By how many generations, I cannot tell," answered Abuela. "But I am sure of who you are."

"How can you be sure?"

Abuela smiled. "By the three stars on your shell, my child." Then the huge sea turtle turned over to show the top of her own shell to Zani. "You see?"

Zani wiped her eyes. Three stars—just like the ancient constellation! "How beautiful!" she exclaimed, "But I've never seen stars like that on my shell."

"You are young, Panzanilla, so they are still dark and distant." Abuela rolled herself back into a comfortable position.

Water sloshed over Zani's shell. She looked over her shoulder to see if the stars were there, and thought maybe she saw two shapes along her spine. If there were three, the last was too far back for her to see.

The pale turtle noticed her looking. "Trust me, my child."

Zani deperately wanted to trust Abuela, especially here in the deep, where there was no one else to trust. So she said, "I will."

Abuela nodded. "You came here, Panzanilla, to the deep. What did you come seeking?"

"I think I have more questions now than before!"

"I understand. But what brought you here?"

"It belched," began Zani awkwardly, "I mean the volcano—it frightened the Island creatures. So, I want to know . . . what do you know of it? Please tell me what you know of the volcano, Abuela."

"Yes, I felt it," she answered. "It woke me from my slumber."

"You must be a good sleeper!"

Abuela's face crinkled up like coral again as she smiled. "The best, my child! But consider this: I live in the deep—the sea is my pillow, the tides my gentle timekeepers, sun and moon only distant memories to me. You might say I am always in a dream."

Zani felt her jaw drop open at Abuela's description of life in the deep.

"Not only will I tell you what I know of the volcano, I will show you the very foundations of the Island."

"Thank you, Abuela!"

"Surely this is why I woke," said Abuela. Slowly she began to sink back into the water. "Follow me, Panzanilla."

Zani took a deep breath and dove into Abuela's wake.

Zani couldn't help but admire the three stars on Abuela's back, glowing bluish-white on her mottled cream and brown shell. Here was Zani's guide to the ancient secrets of the deep. Zani need only follow the stars through the dark waters.

The huge sea turtle's long flippers paddled with power and grace. Swirling water behind them pulled Zani along as the two navigated the great chamber in perfect harmony. A push upward to the ceiling and Abuela's stars now enlightened a vast display of ancient carvings.

She bobbed her head upward so Zani would notice—pictures of a triangle. Then next, cut off at the top with swirls and circles emerging from it—was the birth of the Island—the fiery volcano emerging from the sea. Zani's gaze was still fixed on the scenes above when she felt pulled below. Abuela dove toward an arched doorway, the dark entrance to a descending spiral stairway.

The staircase was narrow enough that Abuela had to tilt her body so her wide flippers could move freely. They swept onward, circling down through the massive structure of interlocking stones. The spiral seemed to unwind the clock of time itself, until at last Abuela surfaced into another dome of solid stone. There, the two turtles caught their breath in another stale air pocket.

Zani gasped, while Abuela inhaled slowly.

"Breathe deeply, my child."

Zani nodded until she could speak again. "So the ancients saw the volcano rise?"

Abuela nodded. "It seems so. But the sea rose too. In the end, this structure provided shelter for them no more."

"Where did they go?"

"Their escape may be etched in the stones." Abuela

glanced upward. "Or perhaps that knowledge is lost to time. In the deep, not every question is answered."

Zani hung her head.

"We have farther to go, my child. You may yet discover what you seek."

At that, Abuela, sank into the water again, and Zani followed close behind.

Then the bottom dropped out. There was no floor below them—only the ocean depths.

Zani wrapped her flippers around Abuela's wrinkled neck and grabbed on. Though she'd grown up in the sea, Zani had always avoided such bottomless places, often called blue holes.

She felt she was floating in space—holding onto the ancient turtle constellation herself.

Abuela banked away from the emptiness, back toward the Island's foundation. There, steep rock walls, covered in porous black rock filled their vision. The sea warmed and they saw an orange glow in the black rock as if the lava awaited its opportunity to escape. Zani's eyes opened wide in alarm, but Abuela simply blinked. It calmed Zani to see Abuela at peace with the sight of fire in the water.

The great turtle's huge flippers flapped like a pelican flying in slow motion. The two swam by the ancient stone structure. Outside, the walls were even more impressive in the ocean blue light, as if stones held up the Island itself. Timeless, permanent, except where some boulder had scraped the wall's surface in its tumble into the sea, a pitiful attempt to fill the deep blue hole.

Eventually they passed the stone gateway, the very entrance Zani had taken. Would they pause for air? Zani remembered how long it had taken her to swim to it before. But Abuela continued without stopping. Zani hoped those long graceful flippers would bring them back soon.

She need not have worried, for Abuela moved them forward more quickly than Zani could have imagined. Before long, they entered the cave opening, which extended its broken stalactite teeth into the sea to welcome them back to the Island. Then up through the salt barrier, and above to the lighter, yet murky fresh water of the cave. Zani held onto Abuela as they resurfaced into the starry chamber of glow worms, water pouring off Abuela's great cream and brown mottled shell.

Zani lay there face up and found the familiar "constellation" again—its three stars in their rightful place—above her . . . and reflected below her on Abuela's magnificent shell.

A voice sounded over the water. "I sssmell sssalt of the sssea!"

Zani turned to see Solo approaching them, his tail swirling the water behind him—only his glowing grin above the surface.

CHAPTER 17
CONNECTING DOTS

"*A*buela! Sssoo good to have you back," said the salamander.

"Good to see you again, Solo."

"Just a minute," Zani interrupted. "You two know each other?"

They both nodded and smiled.

"Why didn't you tell me about Abuela then, Solo?" asked Zani.

Solo shrugged. "I thought it bessst you find each other in your own way."

"A good choice," Abuela agreed. "Discovery is better than description."

"Essspecially when I describe things by sssmell."

"I suppose you're right," Zani admitted. "It seems you see things in a whole different light." Suddenly she knew she'd said that wrong.

"Yesss," Solo smiled. "It's called the dark."

Abuela's face crinkled into a smile. "Never under-estimate Solo!" she said. "He's far more capable than you might expect. He could surprise you."

"He already has," said Zani. "He was the one who told me about the stars that made up the turtle constellation in ancient days."

"Did he now?" aked Abuela. "So you did not keep *all* our secrets?"

Solo shook his head. "I'm sure I ssseem like a ssstrange sssource when it comes to the ssstars."

Zani had to admit he did. "Yes, but everything you said, it was confirmed in the deep."

"A strange place to look for constellations, is it not?" Abuela added. "Under the sea?"

Zani just scrunched her face and glanced up toward the glow worms on the cavern ceiling. "I suppose I've already found more than I came looking for. And yet not all my questions are answered."

"What answers do you still seek, my child?"

"The carvings," Zani asked. "Who made them? Who is the artist?"

"The carvings below were made by the ancients," answered Abuela. "Their names are buried in the past."

"I mean the carvings in the cave, just down the hall from here."

Abuela looked puzzled. "I know not, my child. Do you know about such carvings, Solo?"

Solo dipped his head, like he was about to reveal a secret. "I made them."

"You?" Zani spread her flippers in disbelief. "But you're . . ."

"Blind, right?" the salamander finished the sentence for her.

"You, Solo?" asked Zani. "You are the Artist?"

"Yes," he nodded. "I carved them after listening to Abuela's tales, her descriptions of carvings on the walls of the deep."

"As I said," Abuela repeated, "never understimate Solo."

"But they are not all of ancient times," said Zani.

"Some carvings are of things that have happened just since I came to the Island."

"I guesss you could sssay, I want to keep the tradition going."

Abuela reached her huge flipper around Solo. "Memories keep best underground. What excellent work, my friend!"

"Thank you, Abuela, that meansss a lot when you sssay it."

Silent now, the three floated peacefully in the "starlit" cavern. It was almost like a dream—the glow worms above and their reflection in the still water. Memories of the ancients recorded in the deep, and recent events carved in the cavern halls. Tales of turtles great and small. And perhaps the greatest sea turtle of them all right there, Zani's very own *abuela*.

"Can such a dream last forever in this land of ever-night?" Zani asked herself, her eyes drifting shut at the thought. A smile spread across her face.

Then the alarm went off—the squeaking of a dozen bats or more approaching from the hallway. Silently, Abuela sank just under the water's surface. Perhaps it was to stay out of sight from the bats, lest she frighten them. Or perhaps she merely immersed herself to

106

muffle their squeaks.

"Zani!" squeaked Emilio. "You have reeeturned!"

"Theengs are not good above," another bat screeched.

"Very bad!" agreed another.

"Pleeeese, Zani," Emilio pleaded. "Come and help us. Come now!"

The young sea turtle shook the sleepiness from her head. Then she simply answered, "No."

Even Solo was shocked at her answer. His glowing jaw dropped open.

Emilio made his most urgent appeal. "But weee neeeed you!"

"I want to stay here," said Zani. "I want to stay with Abuela."

CHAPTER 18
TROUBLE ABOVE

Chanty's first crow called the Island creatures to gather by the boulder at the bay. It was his stage, and the strutting rooster made the most of it. He stroked his red comb and paced back and forth as the crowd settled, awaiting his morning cackle. Jajumbee and Boofo hid in the underbrush at the edge of the forest. Who knew what might happen if they dared to show themselves?

A pink sunrise bloomed to replace the purple dawn. Waves lapped gently along the beach of the bay. Creatures from around the Island found their places on the cool sand, with the sun at their back casting long shadows toward Chanty's boulder stage. It seemed a perfect peaceful gathering, that is, until the second crow.

"Cruck-uh-cluckle-doo!" As Chanty tossed back his head, his comb fell artfully to one side. "Good morning Islanders!" He put his wing to one ear and awaited their response.

"Good morning, Chanty."

Chanty furrowed his brow and leaned toward the crowd. "Louder?"

"Good Morning, Chanty!" the Islanders repeated more robustly.

"Let me begin with a simple spelling lesson," said Chanty. He held a piece of charcoal and scrawled a word on the boulder's face so everyone could see.

I S ... L A N D

"Now tell me, what is this?" he asked the group.

A front row lizard raised his hand. "It says Island!"

Chanty nodded. "And what else?"

The creatures scratched their heads, looked at each other nervously, scrunching their faces—but no one dared guess what else Chanty's writing might say.

"It says Island . . . then reading again . . . *is land*."

Some creatures nodded, murmuring in agreement.

"We understand this, don't we?" Chanty raised his regal head and shook the red wattle hanging from his neck. "This Island is *land*. It is *not* the sea."

More knowing nods spread through the crowd.

"You see what I mean? The big, wide sea is out there." He pointed a wing, and several creatures turned to look and consider it. He then strutted back and forth on the boulder until everyone turned back to watch him again. "We're here!" he pulled his feathered fist back toward his chest.

"You're the only 'C' on this Island," said the lizard in the front row.

"Hah! You could say that!" Chanty laughed and strutted until the crowd was like moist sand in his sharp claws. Then he began to shape it.

He spread his beautiful wings skyward. "Look at this Island!" Chanty slowly circled 'round until he faced the volcano. There he stopped and folded his wings. Everyone was silent.

The rooster threw his head back and crowed, "Cruck-uh-bang-gah-boom!" and tossed a fistful of sand and feathers into the air. Shocking! Nearly everyone jumped.

As the creatures resettled themselves, Chanty

strutted, awaiting their full attention.

"What if that had been the volcano? Erupting once more." The rooster let the gravity of the situation set in. Creatures in the front row dusted the sand off their heads.

"Sea creatures? They'd be gone! Disappeared into the deep. Cave creatures? Back under the ground. But what of us?" Chanty furrowed his feathered brow in alarm, "Doomed! No escape for *us*."

The crowd shifted like sand in their seats.

"Would any of them help us?" Chanty shrugged and spread his wings. "No. They would abandon us in a heartbeat! Only fools trust them."

Several nodded their agreement.

"So we need a plan. Our own way of escape." The rooster looked over his shoulder at the volcano again. His tail feathers waved in the morning breeze. The crowd leaned forward, waiting.

He turned back toward the crowd, and announced "I, Chanty, have found a way . . . " He raised his head and put his wings on his hips. ". . . A rescue ship!"

At that news, the crowd buzz started up again.

Chanty held up one wing. "Islanders, yes, a rescue ship is coming! It will anchor in the bay, always at the ready should we need it for our escape from the volcano!" Chanty spread one wing back toward the volcano, then clenched his fist and brought it back to his chest.

There were cheers from the crowd.

"Never again will we be at the mercy of that fiery mountain"—his wings burst upward as if exploding—"or the waters of the sea"—his wings flattened—"or the creatures of the sea." He ended these gestures by moving his wings as if they were the flippers of a sea turtle, and making a silly face.

The crowd laughed. Some clapped and chanted, "Chanty! Chanty! Chanty!"

The rooster just folded his wings and strutted on his stage—occasionally throwing kisses to the Islanders. Then he quieted them once more.

"Today, we gather stores for that ship. Stack them by the edge of the forest, under the shade of the great palm tree, in preparation for that day." Chanty smiled and nodded. "The day our ship comes in!" And the rooster threw back his head and crowed a song of jubilation:

Cruck-uh-cluckle-doodle-doo!

What we see, is what we know,

Island is land—this we crow!

Ocean creatures swim below

Leave us in the lava flow!

We'll be safe with Chanty's tip,

Keep an Island rescue ship!

When comes time for us to go,

Saved from the volcano!

In the underbrush at the edge of the forest, Jajumbee and Boofo backed away from the cheering assembly on the beach.

"He sings." Boofo sighed and put his arm around his gecko friend.

Jajumbee nodded. "A rescue ship seems a strange idea to be coming from a rooster who's never even been on a ship his whole life."

"Another bird brain," croaked Boofo.

114

"Really a bird-brain idea!" agreed Jajumbee.

"Not that bird," added the treefrog, "another bird."

When Jajumbee finally got Boofo's point, he slapped his forehead so hard his fingers stuck.

"Barnacle! Of course!" He shook his fingers off his head. "If that parrot brings a ship here, it sure won't be used to rescue anyone."

CHAPTER 19

OLD NEMESIS

"Let's get going," said Jajumbee.

"Where to?"

"The caves! To see if Zani got anything from the deep."

Boofo scratched his head. "Like what?"

"Like something better than the nonsense Chanty's crowing—something deeper—something true about the Island and the sea!"

"Together!" Boofo croaked.

"Yes, you don't have an island without the sea."

Boofo nodded his agreement.

"Is Land!?" Jajumbee shook his head at its stupidity.

"And this volcano scare," he added, "I only hope Zani can set their minds at ease somehow. I mean, how long has the volcano been there?"

"Always?" Boofo guessed.

"Pretty much," Jajumbee agreed. "Maybe those cave drawings can be explained—made clear."

"Find artist?"

"And perhaps even the answer key to all that's hidden in them?"

"Maybe better songs," said Boofo.

Jajumbee narrowed his eyes at his friend.

"Better than Chanty's!" Boofo clarified.

"I don't think they want to hear me sing anymore," Jajumbee hung his head.

The two turned back into the forest, staying off the trails, hidden beneath the underbrush. They were especially cautious now that Chanty's crowing session was over. The most ambitious of the Islanders were already hunting for food to lay in store for the promised "Rescue Ship."

A flash of feathers above! Jajumbee and Boofo dove into a patch of ferns as they spotted a bird flying overhead just behind them. It was Chanty. Not the most graceful in the air, the rooster flew barely above the treetops, stopping frequently to rest with a commotion of flapping wings and splintering palm leaves.

"Let's follow him," Jajumbee whispered.

Boofo nodded.

The gecko and treefrog scampered from one patch of underbrush to another. Whenever they had to stop, they used their best camouflage skills, blending in with plants, rocks, shells, and flowers along the way.

Chanty kept blustering along his route, leaving a trail of broken vegetation. This floated down to the forest floor like green confetti at his every rest stop.

"Better at strutting," Boofo whispered to his friend.

Jajumbee raised an eyebrow. "Maybe even singing?"

After tracking the clumsy rooster deep into the rainforest, the two friends heard an all too familiar "Caw!" just ahead.

They nodded silently to one another. There was no mistaking that bird call. It was the pirate parrot, Barnacle. Everyone thought he had long ago departed the Island, but he must have been hiding out, waiting for an opportunity for revenge.

The parrot was plotting to avenge the pirates' humiliating defeat at the hands, wings, and flippers of the Island creatures of land and sea. The seadogs may have left with their tails between their legs last time, but if Barnacle's plan worked, they'd return to even the score.

Chanty tumbled into a palm near the parrot, who simply asked, "My mango?"

The rooster sighed and spread his wings. "So sorry, Mr. B. I forgot."

The parrot ruffled his bright green feathers and snapped his heavy beak at Chanty. "Idiot!"

Chanty flinched at first, but then thought to brag instead. "I made the speech!"

Barnacle's eyes brightened. "Did ye promise 'em a boat?"

"I did." Chanty held his head high and tossed his red comb to one side.

"Well, well, well," Barnacle smiled, "Maybe ye arrr worth yer salt!"

"And they'll stock it with supplies," Chanty cackled with glee. "Coconuts, bananas, and mangoes!"

At that news Barnacle could hardly contain his

120

excitement, rubbing his feathered fingers together in glee. Then thought to add, "Now yer makin' me hungry, ye comb-head!"

"Sorry, Mr. B.," Chanty apologized. "I'll go get you a mango."

"Now that's a good bird," the parrot said.

So Chanty flew away, creating a shower of green confetti at his take-off.

Barnacle brushed himself off, rolled his eyes, and uttered something he'd once heard from a particularly nasty pirate sea dog.

Jajumbee and Boofo looked at each other and wondered. They had the element of surprise. Could they take him down? Capture that feathered pirate?

Boofo nodded. He thought it was worth a try.

So they snuck around beneath the tree behind Barney. Slowly, quietly, they crept up the palm's smooth bark until they were nearly level with him. The parrot had closed his eyes and now snored in a harsh whistle.

Jajumbee and Boofo got themselves into position— ready to leap on the parrot—each to grasp one of his wings. At least, that was their plan.

122

Chapter 20
Birds of a Feather

The gecko and treefrog leapt toward Barnacle's wings, hoping to capture the pirate parrot, but just as they leapt, Chanty crashed into the tree carrying a mango in one claw.

"Caw!" cried Barnacle.

Palms bent back, and mango juice squirted all over Jajumbee and Boofo, making their hands and feet slippery. The would-be heroes slid right off the parrot's feathers and fell onto the forest floor. Green confetti vegetation landed on the now-captives as if celebrating Barnacle's accidental escape.

Once the parrot had regained his balance and un-ruffled his feathers, he stared down at Jajumbee and Boofo below. "Well, lookee here!" He dropped down and pinned the gecko and treefrog to the ground with his claws. "If'n it ain't the singin' lizard and his troublesome two-bit toad!"

Chanty was able to untangle his tailfeathers from the palms at last. He dropped down next to his nefarious accomplice. The rooster tilted his head and eyed the two captives sideways. He clucked in surprise, "Jajumbee? Boofo?"

The two sighed in defeat.

The parrot furrowed his brow. "I don't know whart ye thinks yer doin' here, mates, but ye just ruined my mango!"

"Sorry Mr. B.," answered Chanty.

"Oh, you did yer part with that clumsy landing comb-head. Thwarted their plans!" The parrot pressed the gecko and treefrog further into the sand until they squirmed.

Chanty just kept cocking his head as if he had no idea what to do next. Then he announced, "I'll get another mango." He tossed his head high and launched himself back into the air. More shredded leaves fell.

Barnacle just cackled and shook his head.

Jajumbee had an idea, so he begged, "Whatever you

do to us, Barnacle, please, please don't throw us into the dark cavern by the volcano!"

Boofo looked over to his friend wide-eyed, then he croaked, "Nope. Not there!"

"It might blow up at any time!" said Jajumbee.

"Chanty says so!" agreed Boofo, catching on to the ploy.

But Barnacle just laughed at them. "Har, har, har! That rooster sez whatever I tell him to say. He's the bird brain 'round here. Good at crowin' though . . . and struttin' . . . maybe even sings better than you, lizard! Har, har har!"

"But still," Jajumbee made a wide-eyed face of panic, "the volcano!"

"Stop playin' yer silly games with me, Jumblebee!" Barney scolded him. "You an' I both know nothin's no different than it ever been with that there volcano of yours."

"No rescue ship?" Boofo croaked.

"Oh there'll be a *ship* all right," Barancle grinned, "Them idiot Islanders will load it up with food, then me an' my old crew will blast the beach with more firepower than they'll ever see from that volcano!

Goodbye, Island! We be goin' ta sea without ye."

"Bad plan!" croaked Boofo.

"Oh ya think so, do ya toadstool?" Barney squeezed Boofo, who croaked without trying.

Jajumbee tried another tack. "What about Chanty? The Islanders follow him, not you."

"Who needs him?" The parrot sneered.

"Don't you birds of a feather stick together?" asked Jajumbee.

"Har, har, har! What would I need with them flappin' chickens?" Barney laughed. "Not Chanty, nor his half-scratch mudder, Rose, nor his Lily-livered hen . . . cousin . . . er whatever she be. Best use of 'em be cookin' 'em in a pot a soup. Har, har . . ."

Thwack! Out of the blue, a mango smacked Barnacle on the side of his beak. It snapped his head around, rolling him head over heels into the sand. He landed upside-down in a heap of ruffled feathers.

Chanty dropped on him hard, clasping the parrot's feet down and grasping him by the neck in a strangle-hold.

Barnacle shook himself and squawked at Chanty, "Get offa' me, ya comb-head!"

The rooster just narrowed his eyes and replied, "Not a chance, Mr. Bee-brain! You're never telling me what to do. Never again!"

Jajumbee and Boofo got up, brushed the sand off and welcomed Chanty.

"I'm soo sorry!" Chanty clucked. "Looks like I played the fool."

"At least you came back in time," said Jajumbee. "Thank you!"

Still rubbing his throat, Boofo agreed, nodding.

"Oh, yer too late," sneered the pinned parrot. "The pirate ship's already on her way!"

"I'll tell them to fight those invading pirates," Chanty declared, puffing out his chest feathers.

"Sure," Barnacle mocked him. "You can just dash their hopes of rescue with a word! An' the volcano— no problemo!"

The others frowned. Unfortunately, the pirate parrot had a point. A lot had to change about the way the Islanders were thinking, and it had to change in a hurry, before that ship came in.

Barnacle just grinned. He might be on the bottom now, but maybe he'd still come out on top.

"What'll we do with him?" Chanty asked the other two.

"Take him to the bat's cavern," answered Jajumbee. "They'll find a place to keep him out of trouble for a while."

"Good plan," croaked Boofo.

So the three tied the parrot up with a vine, looping it around one leg. Then they tied a coconut onto the end of the vine, so Barnacle needed to drag it through the sand behind him. Tied up and weighted down, Barnacle had no choice but to go with them to be held prisoner by the bats in the cave.

But when they arrived at the mouth of the cave, would Barnacle make one last desperate attempt to escape?

CHAPTER 21

SHORT TREE / BAT'S DOOR

No bats awaited their arrival, so Boofo prepared to call them. He flexed his throat, tried to clear it, but it was still sore from being pinned down by the parrot.

"Umm-Ummm." Boofo tried again. "No luck."

"What's the matter?" asked Barnacle grinning. "Frog in yer throat?"

Boofo just looked away. Then Chanty stepped forward—leaning over the edge of the cave's mouth, "I'll call them," he said, then lifted his head and took a deep breath.

But as the rooster was preparing to crow, Barnacle took his chance. The parrot spun around and used the vine as a sling. The coconut swung right into Chanty's feet, and knocked him into the cave!

Cruck-uh-cluckle-dooooooooo . . .

Down tumbled the rooster, flapping his feathers every which way into the dark.

"Caw!" Emboldened by this success, Barnacle attempted another spin move to knock the others into the cave too.

But both frog and gecko were too quick for him. They hopped out of range, so the swing and miss backfired on the parrot. The coconut pulled him into the cave instead. In fact, the vine wrapped around the palm tree trunk and left Barnacle hanging upside down by one foot. He cawed louder than ever!

"CAW! CAW! CAW!"

The noise woke up all the bats. Dozens of them surrounded the two newcomers to the cave.

Chanty was groaning and rubbing his leg.

"What's going on?" asked one bat.

The gecko and treefrog peered over the edge. Jajumbee called down to the bats, "Sorry to bother you so early, but we've got ourselves a prisoner."

"Or two?" asked another bat.

"Just one," replied Jajumbee. "Chanty rescued us

from that pirate parrot!"

Many bats seemed confused at the news, but glad to hear it nevertheless.

Barnacle, still hanging from one foot, squawked his disgust. "CAW!"

"Chanty," Jajumbee called down, "are you OK?"

"Hmmm, I'm not sure," the rooster answered, "Mr. B—er, Barnacle—hit me pretty hard with that coconut. Twisted my leg landing, too."

"Can you fly out?"

"We can help you." A couple of bats offered.

"Thanks."

But first came a screeching from farther back in the cave. A group of bats, led by Emilio, burst into the chamber. Excited echoes bounced off the walls as the bats circled around and landed on the floor where several had already gathered.

"Bad news," Emilio announced. "Zani won't come back!"

"What?" both Jajumbee and Boofo could hardly believe their ears.

"Oh, you're up there," Emilio looked up. He saw

them and noticed Barnacle hanging by one foot from the palm tree. "Um . . . what?" Then he saw Chanty stand up with the help of two bats, one on each side. "Again, what? Pleeese help me out here. What eeez going on? And eez that Barnacle, the parrot?"

"Pirate, too," croaked Boofo.

"Yes, he's caused all kinds of problems!" said Jajumbee.

"Me too," admitted Chanty, bowing his head. "I'm so sorry."

Emilio looked confused.

"Well," Jajumbee said, "I'll explain later. But first tell us, what's going on with Zani? We could really use her help!"

"Zani met her *abuela*—her grandmother—down below. Now she wants to stay in the deep."

"Uh-oh," croaked Boofo.

Jajumbee nodded and called down to Emilio, "Do you know . . . did she learn something about the volcano? About the Island itself? Some truth of the deep? Because that might help right now."

Emilio considered his answer, scratching his furry head, "Zani said some strange theeengs! Deeper things

132

than bats would know."

A flicker of hope passed between the two friends above.

At last Jajumbee asked, "Can you take us to her, Emilio?"

"Yes, I can try." So Emilio flew up to the entrance, landing on the palm just in front of them. "Hop on," the bat invited them. "Then hold on!"

As they got a good grip for the flight, it was the parrot, Barnacle that had the last word.

"Ye think they'll listen to a sea turtle? Never!" he cackled, "Or gecko songs—with his face on that fearsome volcano? Har, hardy, har! An' they ain't about to listen to no lame rooster what can't make up his bird-brain-mind neither!"

"Hurry!" Boofo urged Emilio. And the three circled out of the chamber in a "pitter-patter." But down the cave's hallway, even over the emptiness of the narrows, they could still hear haunting echoes of the parrot pirate's laugh.

CHAPTER 22

ZANI'S ANSWER

Emilio used his sonar to navigate through the cavern maze in the pitch blackness. At every dodge and every dip, Jajumbee and Boofo saw nothing—but they imagined just missing a stalactite, a stalagmite, or a full column of stone. An orange glow flashed by their side, its rippled reflection reminding them of flowing lava. Then at last, the glowing chamber of living constellations opened up before them. They scanned the surface of the water as Emilio flew a spiral around the underground lake. Where was Zani?

Squinting his eyes in the dim light, Boofo pointed to what looked like a pale boulder just under the surface of the water, "There! Turtle-shaped!"

135

Jajumbee was about to object—it was too large to be a living creature—but then again . . . maybe? Emilio circled back for a closer look and hovered over the spot. Bubbles surfaced from just below it.

"Zani?" called Jajumbee. "Are you there?"

She emerged from under cover, and paddled up to the surface.

"So you've come for me?" Zani asked.

"Yes!" answered Jajumbee, and Boofo nodded his agreement.

"I want to stay here in the deep."

Jajumbee continued uncertainly, "Well, uh . . . can we talk about it?"

"I suppose you won't leave until we do."

Boofo shook his head.

"All right," Zani agreed. "Then we might as well be comfortable."

Emilio, still flapping his gray wings in place, heartily agreed.

So Zani reached down a flipper and tapped the white "boulder" below her. It began to rise, for of course, it was actually Abuela's massive shell. As the

136

water spilled off the sides, Zani perched herself in the center. Emilio landed next to her, and his two riders, Jajumbee and Boofo dismounted. But the three of them could barely take their eyes off the shell they all now stood upon.

"This is Abuela." Zani looked over her shoulder and called, "Abuela, these are my friends . . ." The turtle's great white head rose from the water and turned a huge eye in their direction. "Pleased to meet you." Her voice sounded older than time itself.

Each of the friends introduced themselves, bowing as before royalty.

"Jajumbee, at your service."

"Boofo."

"I am Emilio. Pleeeased to meeet you, too." The bat spread his wings like a cape.

Abuela crinkled her face into a coral-like smile.

"She's not a queen," Zani smiled. "Her name means grandmother."

"Your grandmother?" asked Jajumbee.

"Yes—with who knows how many 'greats' up front?"

"So many have come from the surface." Abuela cocked her head. "Is there trouble above?"

"Yes, madam," replied Jajumbee. "Much trouble."

"All quiet below," said Zani, "under the living stars." She lifted her flippers to the ceiling of glow worms. One dropped and plopped into the lake, making a circle of ripples. Reflections twinkled like the true night sky. Then the fallen glow worm vanished.

"My cousin Solo," Boofo croaked. "He lives here."

Zani chuckled. "That's right, Boofo, you must be sure to greet him before you leave."

Jajumbee rubbed his neck and finally had the courage to say, "We're not leaving without you, Zani."

"But you must sing your songs, Jajumbee. You have to sing!"

Boofo looked sadly over at Jajumbee, who hung his head and said, "No more."

Zani looked confused, "Have you lost your voice?"

"No," the gecko replied, "I have lost my place to another."

"But no one could ever take your place, Jajumbee!"

"Chanty," said Boofo. "He sings." Then corrected

138

himself, "He sang."

"What's going on up there?"

"A pirate ship eez coming," said Emilio.

"Then the Island creatures will fight them off again!" Zani declared.

"No," said Jajumbee. "They invited the ship. Barnacle and crew fooled the creatures of the Island."

"With Chanty's songs," added Boofo.

"You see," Jajumbee continued, "they are now fearful of the volcano, and want a 'Rescue Ship' so they can leave the Island—like the sea creatures could disappear into the ocean and be safe from the mountain's fire."

At that, Abuela's face lost its crinkle and she shook her head sadly. "There is no safety in the ocean depths —not for creatures of the land. Much can be lost in the deep."

"They would never even get on the ship," said Jajumbee. "The pirates will only use the trick to stock up their food stores, then leave the Island behind."

"Can't you sing some sense into them, Jajumbee?" asked Zani.

"They no longer trust me, or Boofo, or any creatures from the sea, or from the caves below." He shook his head. Emilio nodded sadly, too.

Zani replied, "That counts me out then—I'm from the sea and now I'm from the caves too!"

"But did you find answers?" asked the gecko. "Answers from the deep?"

Zani crawled over and stretched her flippers around the huge turtle's neck. "I found Abuela," she said. "I found my family."

Jajumbee sighed and considered the two turtles' embrace. He paused a long while before he finally said, "Zani, I could never ask you to leave Abuela."

There was a long awkward silence. At last, Emilio unfolded his wings, and bent over to allow Jajumbee and Boofo to get on his back once again.

Jajumbee said, "Good bye then, Zani, Abuela. May the constellation Panzanilla—the great turtle—ever shine over your happy home below."

And with that, the bat, the gecko, and the treefrog flew away into the darkness.

CHAPTER 23

THE ARTIST

Jajumbee and Boofo could hardly make sense of it all. They were dizzy from Emilio's dodging obstacles, and wet from the dripping pitter patter of the cave chamber. Emilio even seemed a bit frazzled. Then suddenly the bat put his air brakes on full and crash-landed, sliding along the rippling creek on the hallway floor.

"What in the . . . ?" cried Jajumbee.

Emilio folded his wings so his two riders could see what he saw. Just ahead—a glowing mouth along the wall—moving toward them.

"Solo?" croaked Boofo.

"Surprised to seee you here," added Emilio, brushing himself off once his riders had dismounted.

"Oh, my!" the salamander sniffed, then responded, "Ssso you have dissscovered my ssssecret."

"Your secret?" asked Jajumbee. He noticed the sharp, black rock in Solo's hand. "Wait—you? You are the artist, Solo?"

"Solo!" croaked Boofo.

"Yessss, it'ssss me."

"But . . . but you can't see," said Jajumbee. "How? How do you do this?"

Before Solo could form an explanation, Emilio said, "There are many ways of seeing, my friends. Many think weee, thee bats, are blind."

"Sssso right, Emilio." Solo held out his fingers so his glowing smile lit them. "Mostly, these are my eyesss."

"But how do you know what to draw?"

"Carve," Solo corrected the gecko, then explained, "I lisssten to tales of the deep. If a ssstory is well told, it can open eyesss in your mind." He touched his fingers to his head.

"Abuela?" asked Boofo.

"Yesssss. The ancient turtle of the ssssea. I see much through her sstories." Solo nodded. "She takessss time to tell them well. Then I carve them here, sssso I can remember."

"Have we forgotten these ancient stories of the deep, Solo?" Jajumbee asked.

"Possssibly," he answered. "It would ssseem ssso. Under the sky above, many are losssst in the moment. They know ssso little of the Island's deep passst."

Jajumbee scratched his chin. "Well, they think they are running out of time!"

Solo nodded. "Ssseee? It's a problem of perspective." The salamander then felt the wall and found the place where he'd just stopped carving. "Close your eyesss and look here, cousssin!" He reached for Boofo's hand and traced the frog's fingers over the scene. Then asked him, "What did you just sssee?"

"The volcano," said Boofo.

"Was it ex-sssploding?"

"Did not . . . see." Boofo admitted. He was about to peek, when Solo reached to cover his cousin's eyes. The salamander smiled his glow-worm smile. "Ssso . . . now you sssee."

Boofo cocked his head.

"Sssome wish to ssee what they cannot know," said Solo. "Ssso, they ssee what they expect to sssee."

"And they beecome blind to everytheeeng else," Emilio added. It seemed bats could understand "seeing things without seeing them" better than most.

"I see what you mean!" Jajumbee exclaimed.

Boofo held up his hands and croaked, "I see, too!"

Solo's smile glowed brighter than ever. "Indeed you do, cousin!"

Jajumbee rubbed his chin again. "We need these stories . . . these ancient tales . . . they need to be told to the creatures above."

"Those under the sssun do not sssee?"

"No." Jajumbee shook his head. "Not now."

"Then tell them," Solo said. "Sssing them a sssong, Jajumbee!"

"No listen," Boofo said.

"Ssso sssorry."

"We need help," the gecko admitted.

"Abuela?" offered Boofo.

"Abuela is not ssseen above," said Solo. "She finds peace in the deep."

"Like Zani," Boofo sighed.

Jajumbee asked, "Will you help us then?"

The artist leaned his hand on the carving of the volcano and traced a sleepy plume of smoke above it. "I will ssssee what I can do," he said at last.

"That's all we can ask." Jajumbee, put his arm around the salamander's shoulder.

So it was agreed that Solo would ride on Emilio's back, and the others would follow close behind to the bats' chamber. It wasn't much farther.

Awaiting them there, a rather lame and humbled rooster likely wondered if there was anything he could do to make up for all the trouble he'd caused the Island —the only home he'd ever known. And also, there was an angry captive parrot, who probably was doing his best to assure Chanty that, no, there was nothing.

CHAPTER 24

STAGE PERFORMANCE

Emilio kept a close eye on Barnacle—who was now barricaded behind stone columns. So the four others prepared one last attempt to turn the tide of Islander opinion. It seemed a sorry lot: a rooster who had lost his strut, a cave salamander who had lost his sight, a treefrog who was short on syllables, and a gecko who had lost his singing voice. They discussed a plan as they made their way through the forest toward the stage at the bay.

"I suppose it should begin with crowing," Chanty ventured. "They're used to that."

"Can you get up on that rock without help?" asked Jajumbee. "That's a bad limp you've got."

"I have to try."

"Then you next, Jajumbee?" asked Solo.

"No, I think you better be next, Solo." Jajumbee grimaced. "They don't think much of me. I'm a friend of sea creatures, and they say it's my face on that 'dangerous' volcano."

"Sssso, you want me to tell the ssstory I told you?" asked Solo.

"Sure, maybe draw . . ."

"Carve," Solo corrected him.

" . . . carve on the rock stage, have Boofo do his thing, like you did in the cave."

But Boofo wasn't sure. "Too many!"

"I'm sure you can do it, Boofo! Emilio said you gave a great speech to hundreds of bats."

"Too many faces," Boofo muttered to himself. "Angry faces."

"Then you, Jajumbee?" asked Solo again.

The gecko hung his head. "Maybe Chanty can start a song."

"No," the rooster objected. " Everyone needs to see you, Jajumbee—hear your voice again."

But Jajumbee did not answer.

They approached the rock stage from behind, so only Chanty would be seen at first.

The rooster struggled to pull himself on stage, grunting, feathers flapping, his comb uncombed.

Two lizards noticed it and seemed puzzled. "What's wrong with Chanty?"

But he managed a pretty good crow all the same.

So the Islanders gathered in the sand around, smiling, whispering, and nodding. It seemed they expected good news.

Whispers were heard all around, "The rescue ship!"

"The ship!"

"It's coming!"

"I saw it myself," claimed a spindly crab with freakishly long eye stalks, "still distant on the horizon."

But his friend, Carlos, grumbled, "Never liked ships." It seemed the shipwreck over his favorite hole in the beach still stuck in his crawdad.

Chanty crowed again.

Cruck-uh-cluckle-doodle-doo!

Then the rooster swallowed hard and took a limping step or two across the stage.

"My dear Islanders," he began.

A lizard in the front row responded with "Island is land! Island is land!" And a chant began to gain volume among the crowd.

Chanty spread his wings, a gesture for them to stop chanting. Then he began again. "All creatures of the Island, indeed a ship is coming . . ."

"Res-cue ship! Res-cue ship! Res-cue ship!" Another chant.

Again Chanty spread his wings. He shook his head, red comb flopping. They finally stopped, and Chanty tried again. "The ship will not rescue us!" he declared.

Well, that started quite a commotion in the crowd. Murmurs spread over them like a wave.

"Please listen," shouted Chanty. "We will need no rescue! Our life is here, on the Island."

"That's crazy talk, Chanty!" yelled a lizard in the front row. "You promised us a rescue ship!"

He held up his wings, asking their attention again, "Let me . . . let us . . . explain what's wrong." Chanty waved Solo and Boofo up to the stage. "These two cousins will tell . . . and show . . . us an ancient story," he announced, "an ancient story from the deep!"

A few in the crowd recognized Solo, and almost everyone knew Boofo.

"I didn't know they were cousins," said the lizard in the front row. That seemed enough a distraction for Solo and Boofo to begin their act. As the salamander carved the shape of the volcano, all eyes focused on the stage stone. As in the cave, Boofo closed his eyes and traced over the shape, hesitating at the top.

Would Solo draw lava bursting out of it to cover the Island in fire and ash? No. Instead he covered Boofo's eyes, and led the frog's hand peacefully down the opposite slope. But as soon as Solo opened his mouth to explain, the glow-worm glow shown like a spotlight and a great commotion arose from the crowd.

"It glows!" shouted the lizard in the first row, "Like lava!"

"Lava!"

"Fire from below!"

"Fire!"

Soon the crowd was so worked up, they would not even quiet for Chanty, who shook his wattle and raised his wings high and wide.

Then Jajumbee had a thought—a song? Nothing else seemed to be working!

The gecko stayed behind the stage, not daring to show his volcanic face. But still, he sang:

Bat in thee cave, an fish in the school

—Nobody play the Island fool!

Frogs hopping 'round on mo-skee-to fuel

—Nobody play the Island fool!

Ship sailing into the Island bay

—Nobody play the Island fool!

Rescue nobody. Just hear what we say

—Nobody play the Island fool!

Stay with volcano,

Es no problemo,

Always the same-o!

152

No play this game—NO!

—Nobody play the Island fool!

—Nobody play the Island fool!

"Hey, that sounds like the gecko!" said the lizard in the front row.

"Jajumbee!"

"The face of the volcano!"

"He *became* the volcano!" declared the lizard.

"It's a trick!"

The Islanders stood up and crowded toward the stage.

Jajumbee hopped up onto the rock and declared, "It is no trick! I am here! I am *not* the volcano!" He could think of nothing else to say.

It did not work. The crowd was angry! Islanders rushed toward the stage. Some picked up sticks or shells and hurled them at the four on the rock.

"Take Solo," Jajumbee called to Chanty, "and fly! Now!"

The rooster grabbed the cave salamander with his

good leg, and flapped clumsily into the air. Feathers fluttered behind him as he barely got high enough to clear the first palm tree. Jajumbee and Boofo dove into the underbrush and ran after them into the forest.

CHAPTER 25
ANCIENT TALE

Down in the quiet lower chamber, Zani swam peacefully under the "living stars." She yawned and asked Abuela to tell her a story—a tale of ancient days.

Abuela's face crinkled like coral. There was nothing she enjoyed doing more.

She started, "Look up at the three glow worms, those three in a row, my child."

Zani scanned the ceiling. They were still there.

"What are they?" Abuela quizzed her.

"Why, those are the stars of the ancient turtle constellation," Zani declared, and giggled. "Though Jajumbee called them the constellation Panzanilla!"

"Did he?"

"He did."

"Then he must believe you capable of great things," said Abuela, "even as the turtle of the ancient tale itself."

"Tell me the tale, Abuela."

The giant sea turtle took a deep breath as Zani settled onto her shell to gaze upward. Then Abuela began, "It was told long ago, that before all else, there was a turtle—a creature strong enough to carry the world upon its back."

"Do you believe it's true?"

"I simply tell the tale, my child. And you simply listen."

"Sorry for interrupting," Zani apologized.

Abuela continued, "The first turtle that was ever told this tale believed it. And he became proud. In fact, he was intolerable toward the other animals. He did not like looking up at them. He wanted the others to look up to him. One day a heron was hunting for a meal along the shore. Seeing the turtle squirming in the sand, she stabbed at him—striking his hard shell three times. Safely inside, the turtle laughed, bragging that no heron could ever harm him. At that, the bird grabbed the entire turtle shell in her beak, and launched into the air. She flew high into the evening sky. When the turtle looked down, he saw all other animals below him. It was just as he had wished, except for one thing. They did not look up at him. Then he wondered what he would see if he looked up from this height."

"He saw the stars, didn't he?"

"Yes, my child. And he was humbled. For those stars appeared as a great shell that encircled all the earth. The turtle now knew that even if he had carried the earth on his back as the most ancient tales told—he would still be but a small creature amid the stars. The fiery stars would always be above him."

Zani wondered a while, then asked, "What great things did he accomplish?"

"He came to understand what was true about himself by understanding the world in which he lived. That, my child, is the beginning of all great things that have ever been accomplished."

"And he was given a place in the stars."

"So we could know his story," Abuela finished, then gazed at the "living stars" above them. She asked, "Do you know your place in the world, Panzanilla?"

"This is my place," said Zani, "with you, Abuela."

"There are greater stars than these, my child. These are but a reflection of those above."

"You think there are great things for me to do?"

"I do, Panzanilla."

"But you are my family—my grandmother. I want us to be together, Abuela!"

"Then so we shall be."

"Even in great things?"

"Yes, in whatever great deeds are left for me to do, we shall accomplish them together, Panzanilla."

"Those three stars on your shell are still shining," said Zani.

Abuela smiled her crinkly smile.

"Perhaps we have a great thing to accomplish together tonight," offered Zani.

"Perhaps we do, my child, So then, you must tell me that story."

Zani held her head high and declared, "So it begins . . . under the starry sky . . ."

Chapter 26
Ship at Anchor

As the sun began to sink into the sea, the hopes of the Islanders rose. No longer just a rumor spread by the sharpest-eyed creatures—a ship really was sailing toward the Island. They could all see it now, the Rescue Ship. Just like Chanty had said before he came back with an injured leg, with the weird-acting cousins, and "volcano-face" himself—the singer formerly known as Jajumbee.

Meanwhile, Jajumbee and Boofo had found a tall leafy palm tree to hide in, a high perch from which they could watch the ship enter the bay.

"Smooth sailing getting in," said the gecko. "That lava flow really made for an easy entry to the bay. Too bad our first visitors . . ."

"Pirates," Boofo finished the sentence for him.

Jajumbee asked, "Can you see the flag?"

They both strained to see if the *Black Widow* flew her true colors.

"Not black," answered Boofo. "No spider."

"Oh, I see. It's just a white sheet flying from the main mast." Jajumbee squinted. "But there's a red shape drawn on it."

"Heart," croaked Boofo, rolling his eyes.

Jajumbee slapped his hand to his forehead, where, of course, it stuck. He sighed. "That's so fake! Maybe the pirate sea dogs have overplayed their hand. Surely, the Islanders will suspect some mischief is afoot!"

But the next thing they heard was a chant coming from the bay, "Res-cue ship! Res-cue ship! Res-cue ship!" Then there arose a great cheer from the gathering crowd as the *Black Widow*, under a false flag, cast anchor in the bay.

Jajumbee and Boofo just looked at each other and shook their heads.

160

"They just see what they want to see," sighed the gecko.

Boofo didn't say a word. He just nodded and covered his eyes.

The two of them kept watch from their palm tree perch as the sun sank into the sea behind the Island. The Islanders built festive fires along the beach sharing food with the visitors, who didn't look much like pirates. The crew was dressed in tattered white robes, which might have once been a sail. And there weren't that many of them. Jajumbee figured some of the pirates were hiding below the ship's deck, well out of sight.

It was nearly dark, so the bats would come out soon.

"Boofo, can you call Emilio like you did at the mouth of the cave?"

"Think so." The frog cleared his throat, inflated it with air, and made his highest-pitched croak—a sound that only bats could hear. But nobody came.

"Keep calling," said Jajumbee, "He'll hear you."

So he did. Before long they saw a bat flapping over the forest coming their direction. It was indeed Emilio.

"Good to seee you," he squeaked. "We wondered where you went."

"Just watching," replied Jajumbee, "but it doesn't look good."

"Big party," grumbled Boofo, wishing he could at least enjoy some of their food.

"What's your beeeg plan?" asked Emilio.

Jajumbee sighed. "I wish we knew. But whatever we do, I'm sure we can use the help of as many bats as possible."

Emilio replied, "You can count on us."

"Thank you."

The three friends sat quietly in the tree and watched as the Islanders ate and danced with the sailors.

A wooden ramp was stretched from ship to shore. They began to carry food stores on board the ship. There was laughing and celebration all along the bay shore.

Boofo's belly grumbled.

"You can say that again," said Jajumbee.

And Boofo's belly did.

162

Emilio felt so sorry for the hungry frog, that he invited him to fly along on his back to hunt mosquitoes for a while.

"Go ahead, Boofo," said Jajumbee. "I'm sure you'll think better on a full belly."

The treefrog smiled and nodded. He hopped on Emilio's furry back, got a good hold, and off they flew.

Jajumbee sighed, stuck his head in his hands, and wished for a song. But nothing came to mind.

Darkness covered the Island. Soon the stars shone like glow worms above him—a strangely inferior comparison. Jajumbee sprawled out on the treetop, waiting for his friends to return. What a spot for stargazing! And there were the three stars in a row, the ancient turtle constellation. Most called it Orion's Belt, but for Jajumbee, it could only be the constellation Panzanilla, turtle in the sea of stars. But unlike the ancient turtle, Panzanilla's story was still unfinished. Perhaps it needed a song.

Hmmmm-mmm-mmm. Out of the sea,

She came to the Island, and she showed to me

The rules are but shadows of the things that be.

Hmmmm-mmm-mmm. Back to the deep,
She found her dream, and she fell asleep—
Glow worms but shadows of the things that be.

Hmmmm-mmm-mmm. High in the sky,
Three stars in a row, where the turtle did fly
Her story's unfinished . . .

" . . . but why?" Jajumbee stopped, for he did not know what more to sing.

His thoughts were interrupted by a shadow gliding down from the constellations. It was Emilio, with Boofo on his back. The gecko stood up to greet them as they landed next to him on the treetop.

"Catch many mosquitoes?" asked Jajumbee.

Boofo belched. Then turned a brighter orange.

Jajmbee couldn't help but smile. "And they say *I'm* the one who's like the volcano."

Emilio smiled. "It was quite a feast! As good as anything down at the bay tonight."

Boofo nodded in agreement.

164

"So, any idee-uhs, yet?" asked the bat. "Remember, I've got your bats!"

Jajumbee scratched his head and looked up in the sky. "Not quite. But perhaps the answer is still out there somewhere." His eyes refocused on the three stars in a row.

"Maybeee you should reeturn to thee cave. Get some rest," Emilio suggested. "I'll keeep watch here. Eeef anything happens, I'll let you know."

So the two agreed, made their way down the tall palm, and slipped into the dark forest, heading back toward the cave. They found their way by the stars that shone between the leaves of the canopy.

"Good sky hunting," said Boofo, who was so full of mosquitoes that he couldn't help but belch again. "Excuse me." He offered his apology and added a huge yawn.

"You know, Boofo," Jajumbee thought out loud, "maybe the volcano didn't belch as a warning, maybe it was just full, and ready for a long nap."

Boofo blinked slowly. "Like me."

"Exactly." Jajumbee pointed to his friend. "If only the Islanders could see it that way."

"And soon," agreed Boofo, "before 'rescue.' "

"Yes! Before the pirate 'rescue ship' sails away with half the Island's food!"

CHAPTER 27

LOST CAUSE?

By the time Jajumbee and Boofo arrived back at the Short Tree entrance to the cave, many of the bats had already returned. Early for that. All the chatter echoed of one word—"ship."

"The sheep, eeetz heere already!"

"Eeetz flag is a heart!" It made several bats snicker.

"Who would beelieeeve that?"

Chanty sat on a stone with his foot up, shaking his head at the news.

"Glad to see you made it back safely, Chanty," said Jajumbee. "Is Solo OK?"

"He's in back drawing on the walls."

"Carving," Boofo corrected him.

"Right, carving," replied the rooster. "With all that's been happening, I suppose he's got a lot of artwork to catch up on."

"Island stories are happening all around us," agreed Jajumbee. He looked around the cave. "Where's Barnacle?"

"Still sleeping, I hope. We locked him in a stone column cage, just around the corner." Chanty put his wing to his ear. He could hear the parrot's rhythmic whistling. "Yup. Still snoring. He's intolerable when he's awake."

"Always," agreed Boofo.

"You saw the ship, right?" asked the rooster.

Jajumbee nodded.

"Any ideas?"

Jajumbee shook his head.

"Any hope?"

"Always," croaked Boofo.

Chanty hung his head and dipped his tail feathers. "I made such a mess of things."

"We tried to fix it," sighed Jajumbee.

"But lost . . ." Boofo just had to say it, "Lost strut," he gestured to the rooster. "Lost voice," he pointed to himself. "Lost stage," he looked at his friend Jajumbee, and added, "Lost song."

168

"Ouch." The gecko admitted. "You're right, Boofo. And the pirates didn't steal it from us, nobody did—we just lost it ourselves."

The others agreed.

"Let's get it back." Jajumbee stood up and puffed out his chest. "Tonight, we'll make an Island story to remember!"

"Keep Solo drawing for days!" said Chanty, his tail feathers perking up again.

Boofo smiled and added, "Carving." Chanty and Jajumbee laughed together.

"Thanks for the correction, Boofo," added the rooster, "every bit of it!" He tossed his comb to one side and smoothed it down, ruffled his feathers, and said, "Hop on, guys. Let's fly out of here!"

"Up to the stars!" declared Jajumbee. He and Boofo prepared themselves for a wild ride.

Chanty launched toward the short tree, circled around it, knocked against the leaves—creating the usual shower of green confetti—getting every bats' attention. They all followed him out, flying back together toward the bay.

CHAPTER 28
STARRY NIGHT

With the constellation Panzanilla shining high over the bay, Jajumbee, Boofo, Chanty, and a host of bats flew toward it. When they passed over the tallest palm tree, Emilio could hardly believe his eyes.

"Whatever you're doing, wait for meeee!" he squeaked, leaping up to join the rooster-led formation.

Seeing Emilio, Chanty called out, "Take the lead here, circle them 'round the ship in the bay."

"Weee got your bats!" he agreed.

"We lost something down there, but we'll get it back!" called Chanty. "We're heading for the crow's nest, top of the mast. Just keep flying around it."

"Wee hear you!" replied the bat. So they circled in formation, as Chanty made a perfect landing at the crow's nest of the ship.

The bats' flying circle caught everyone's attention—and there in the center of the circle, Chanty spread out his wings, threw back his head, and crowed.

Cruck-uh-cluckle-doodle-doo!

"Islanders and all creatures," the rooster began, "let me give a proper introduction to these white-robed sailors—the crew of our Rescue Ship!"

Everyone cheered and applauded, except the sailors, that is. They wanted to talk about what their "mission of mercy" was, rather than who they were. Maybe they figured the less attention on them, the better.

Chanty smiled down at the creatures on the beach. They seemed glad he was back on board, and were willing to forgive him for the embarrassing stage production earlier that day.

Meanwhile, Jajumbee and Boofo stayed out of sight. Peering through a crack in the crow's nest, they recognized one of the "Rescue Ship" crew, despite his clever attempt at disguise.

"The short one, there on deck," Jajumbee whispered, "It's Pip."

Boofo cocked his head sideways to get a better view through the crack, then nodded his agreement. "No angel," he croaked.

"Even if he is dressed up like one," said Jajumbee. "Remember how he took back the ship?"

"Barnacle helped," Boofo recalled.

"Then he shot Zani to shore like she was a cannon-ball! That scurvy little seadog nearly beat us all!"

"But," Boofo reminded him, "not count chickens!"

"Hah! That's right, Boofo," said Jajumbee. "Never count out the chickens!" He looked up at Chanty. "Not this rooster either!"

Boofo tugged on the rooster's leg. "That's him. That's Pip."

"Call him out," said Jajumbee.

Chanty nodded and lifted his wings to silence the crowd. "Now let me introduce the leader of our rescue ship . . ."

The white-robed seadog tried to slip into the shadows along the rail.

"Come on out, now! There he is! This, my dear Islanders . . ." The rooster would not continue until Pip stood exposed on deck.

"Why this, my dear Islanders—this is none other than Pip—pirate seadog of the *Black Widow!*"

Gasps spread through the crowd on the beach.

Pip suddenly felt trapped. "You bird-brained son of a brooding hen!" He yelled up at the crow's nest. The Islanders looked at each other in shock. What was this?

Chanty nodded, "Like mother, like son." He pointed down at the squirming seadog, "Thought you'd take another shot at us, eh, Pip? You should have known better than to think you could outsmart any rooster born to your old nemesis—my mother, Rose."

As if on cue, Jajumbee and Boofo popped up and peered down at him saying, "Remember us, Pip?"

"You two? Oh, you think you're so clever—back in the crow's nest—just like last time!"

"As I remember, we had the upper hand," Jajumbee reminded him in song.

OoooooOOOoooOOoooooOOo,

Look up toward the sky.

OooooooOOOoooOOoooooooOOo,

And you will hear my cry.

OooooooooOOOoooOOooooooOOooooooo,

Hear your final call,

OooooooooOOOoooOOooooooOOooooooo,

Warning to you all . . .

"All seadogs—on deck!" shouted the furious Pip.

And up from the ship's hold spilled a rag-tag crew of pirate seadogs—just as Jajumbee had suspected. There was the Great Dane, Big Tom, the peg-legged mutt, O'Grady, and even Captain Crag, the crusty old bulldog himself. There stood the most infamous crew members of the *Black Widow.*

"Well, well, well," roared Crag, "If'n it ain't arrr old friends—the singin' gecko and the croakin' treefrog!"

"Good to see you again, Captain Crag!" called Jajumbee. And Boofo waved to him.

"So sorry we can't stay an' chat a while, mates," Crag replied, "but we got arrselves a cargo full of Island food, an' we'll be leavin' whiles it's still fresh and delicious. And before that volcano blows its top!"

Well, that set everyone into a quandary. What should they do? Go with the pirates to get away from the volcano? The whole crowd of Islanders looked confused and ash-faced fearful.

"Nobody's going with you," Jajumbee called down to the seadogs, "because you're not leaving, not just yet."

"An' just who's gonna stop us?" bellowed Crag.

"That's easy," answered Chanty. "We even drew a circle for you." He spread his wings, lifting his head toward the circle of bats flying above them.

"You three?" Crag threw his head back and laughed. "It'll take more than three to stop us." Then Crag looked over the frightened crowd along the beach, adding, "I don't think you got much help around here this time. Just a bunch of sandy-toed land-lubbers!"

Crag crossed his arms on his chest and scowled a fearsome scowl. "Load the cannon, Pip. Tom, O'Grady, get ready to weigh anchor. We're sailing out with the goods!"

The crew went to obey their orders when . . .

CRASH!

176

Splinters exploded around the bow as the ship lurched right up out of the water!

All the seadogs hit the deck. O'Grady howled—his pegleg splintered from the crash.

Then down the ship plunged, making enough waves to wash out the campfires along the bayside. The Islanders screamed and fled into the underbrush, up trees, and behind rocks.

"WHARRRT was that?" Crag yelled, picking himself up off the deck.

Pip was half-covered in gunpowder from the barrel tipping over on him.

And Big Tom? He was hanging over the rail.

But up in the crow's nest—Jajumbee, Boofo, and Chanty had safely braced themselves for the impact. From their high perch, they'd seen it coming. Moving directly toward the ship, what looked like a huge white boulder just under the water's surface—a turtle shell, with three glowing stars.

"Abuela," Jajumbee said, "she came to help us!"

Then everyone heard a great creaking sound as the ship tilted, cracked, and then the "rescue ship" began to sink.

"To the lifeboat!" bellowed Crag. So the pirate seadogs all scrambled into an overcrowded boat that was nearly lowered into the bay already. The ship was sinking so fast!

All was chaos! Pirates cursed, Islanders screamed, and gurgling water filled the hold. But the last great sound that everyone heard? It was the bay swallowing the pirate ship up with a resounding belch.

"Hey, that sounded like the volcano!" laughed Jajumbee.

"And me," croaked Boofo with a sly smile.

Chanty just looked around and wondered, "Have you ever seen such a huge turtle?"

"Oh yes," replied the smug gecko, "even bigger."

"Where?"

"That's easy," answered Jajumbee. He pointed up to the circle of bats. "Up there—we even drew a circle for you."

"Huh?"

"Three stars . . . in a row," said Boofo.

"'That's right," added Jajumbee, "the ancient turtle constellation."

178

"Really?" Chanty gazed up to the distinctive line of stars. "What's it called?"

"I like to call it the constellation Panzanilla."

By then the flying circle was breaking up into individual bats, who now joined them, hanging from the edge of the crow's nest to rest. With the ship settled at the bottom of the bay, its mast now rose only a few feet above the water's surface.

Emilio landed there with the others and folded his wings. "Whew, I was beegining to theenk you would never stop talking, while wee just circled and circled, and . . ."

The three laughed. "Our apologies, Emilio," Jajumbee offered.

"Eeetz OK. Somebody's got to circle thee answers."

"That's right. Otherwise, we might not know where to look," said Jajumbee. "Up, down, or sometimes . . . the answer is right in front of our eyes."

"Or maybe," croaked Boofo, "it comes from the deep."

"Did someone call me?" A sea turtle head popped up from under the water.

"Zani! So good to see you again!" cried Jajumbee.

"Good to see you too," answered Zani. "I figured we had more stories still to be written."

"And more pictures for Solo to draw on the cave walls," added Chanty.

"Carve," Boofo corrected him.

"Of course!" replied the rooster. "There should be plenty more cave carvings of turtles soon! You think so, Zani?"

But there was no answer from the sea turtle. For Zani was gazing at the turtle in the stars.

CHAPTER 29

BAY PLAY

Around the bay, Islanders fled from the wreckage that Abuela brought upon the *Black Widow,* and now peered out from their hiding places. Their "Rescue Ship" had been swallowed up by the bay, followed by a huge belch. What a surprising turn of events!

Boofo noticed all the creatures watching, waiting to see would come next. He motioned to Jajumbee, and croaked, "Out there . . . many eyes . . . ears."

"We owe them an explanation," said Jajumbee.

"Owe them? They were chasing us into the forest earlier today," Chanty reminded them.

"Nobody wants to admit they played the fool," said Jajumbee. "That's what I told them. That's why they chased me away."

Boofo raised his eyebrows and whispered, "But . . . they did."

"Everybody plays the fool . . . sometimes," said Zani. "Maybe even by hiding down below—like I did—when you needed me most."

"A lot of foolishness went on, and we all played our part," said Jajumbee.

Chanty and Boofo both hung their heads. They had to agree.

"Perhaps what we owe them," said Jajumbee, "and what they owe us in return . . . is respect."

Suddenly a coconut popped up from underwater—right into Zani's shell—bonk!

"Ooof!" the sea turtle exclaimed, "And a share in the celebration of our . . . the whole Island's . . . victory!"

Another coconut surfaced, and another! Up popped a trio of mangoes, two bunches of bananas! Fruit was popping up everywhere!

Chanty raised his head in celebration.

Cruck-uh-cluckle-doodle-doo!

The rooster spread his wings in an open invitation, "Come on in, everyone! The water's delicious!"

And all around the bay, one Island creature after another jumped into the bay to join in the celebration. Hummingbirds perched on mangoes, sucking the sweet nectar with their beaks. Crabs perched on bunches of bananas, waving one in each claw. And there—on a floating coconut—the lizard from the front row was dancing!

Zani offered rides on the back of her shell to those too small to swim. Then the bats got into the act as well, giving rides to the most adventurous among them—flying, swooping, diving, even snatching fruit from the surface—bobbing for mangoes!

The three in the crow's nest danced around the circle, Chanty hopping on one leg. Before long Boofo had to stop, rubbing his belly full of mosquitoes.

Jajumbee rested with his friend. They gazed up at the stars, as the white sheet flag with its hand-drawn heart flapped gently over them.

"You know, maybe that heart flag wasn't so silly after all," Jajumbee smiled.

"Perfect," agreed Boofo. Then he turned to his friend and scrunched his face. "But something missing."

"What?" asked Jajumbee, "What could make this night more perfect?"

Boofo smiled. "Gecko song."

Jajumbee couldn't help but agree.

Dig, dig, dig-uh-boom-bah-ay!

Seadogs, they say good-bye-ay!

Ship sinks, rests here in our bay,

Fruit floats, popping up our way!

Big belch—that's what the bay say!

Ooh, dig, dig, dig-uh-boom-bah-ay!

Livin'—livin' the Isle way,

Who knows, what comes the next day?

No one, no matter what say,

So live—livin' the Isle way!

Zani took a break from giving rides around the bay to crawl into the crow's nest and join her friends. "Nice to hear you singing again." She gave Jajumbee a full two flipper hug.

"Seems like we all found our voices again," he answered, nodding Boofo's way, though the treefrog's eyes were closed.

"And looks like somebody got their strut back," Zani added, seeing Chanty still hopping and flapping his way around the crow's nest circle, feathers flying.

"Better moves," croaked Boofo.

"I thought you were asleep," said Zani.

"Nope," he croaked. "Admiring stars."

"Which ones?" asked Jajumbee.

"You know," the treefrog grinned, "those three."

"Those stars," Zani agreed, "they're the real deal."

The three gazed up at the familiar three-star turtle constellation . . . and it seemed, it twinkled right back at them.

Exploring Themes under the Surface

The Mysteries of Pattern Recognition—The story begins with a question of pattern recognition. It seems an image of Jajumbee's face has appeared on the top of the Island's volcano. But can natural processes form patterns that appear to be something so recognizable? Was this a coincidence, or was Jajumbee being summoned to some greater purpose by design?

At first, Jajumbee dismisses the notion that the volcanic formation has any meaning, saying that our eyes see patterns in nature all the time—pointing to the waves of the sea. Then Carlos notes that the turtle-like wave Jajumbee declared to be nothing more than a wave, was actually Zani the sea turtle swimming to shore.

The theme develops further as Jajumbee and Zani go underground to study the cave drawings. The scenes seem to reveal secrets about the Island's history. Additionally, those scenes contain hidden objects—familiar things between other shapes or nested within patterns—hidden right before their eyes. Perhaps those are clues with their own hidden meanings?

Deeper in the caves the glow worms are arranged on the ceiling in patterns which resemble constellations in the night sky. One familiar constellation, Orion's Belt, represented a turtle in ancient Mayan culture. Could that mean something to the sea turtle, Panzanilla? How can a constellation look like two different things? How does it even look like a pattern at all? Yet generations have told stories from these patterns in the stars—some of the oldest stories in the world.

The Senses—With much of the story taking place in the dark, characters often use senses other than sight. Bats use their excellent hearing to guide them with sonar squeaks through dark caves and to capture mosquitoes at night. Solo, the blind salamander uses his enhanced senses of smell and touch in surprising ways to help reveal secrets of the Island. Underground, squeaky echoes and salty smells offer far more reliable information than what can be seen by the flickering light of a torch, or the dim glow of a worm.

Fire & Water— The integration of Island and sea is a central theme in the story. A volcanic island is the very essence of fire within water. Both elements pose distinct advantages and dangers to the creatures of both environments. What are they? In nature, fire and water tend to keep each other in check. Even so, the creatures of each environment must learn over again to appreciate the value of each other's natural environment in a bigger picture of their world. In the process, Jajumbee and Zani follow a *thalweg* through a *lava tube,* before they must part ways at the *halocline.*

Time— Separated from nature's familiar time keepers—the daily cycle of the sun, moon, and stars—it may seem that time passes slowly underground. Zani finds that sense of timelessness comforting, retreating into its dream-like stillness even in the face of her friends' peril. The deep is a storage vault of the past, with creatures and stories yet undiscovered. But it keeps its secrets well.

Trust— *The Island Rules?* is fundamentally a story about trust. Who should be trusted? Can our trust be misplaced by a clever use of manipulation? How can trust be regained once lost? Jajumbee and Boofo both face this special challenge—losing trust even in themselves, and each one's ability to make a difference in their world. Each needs to face their own perceived limitations in order to restore the harmony of the Island.

Made in the USA
Middletown, DE
09 March 2025